The Endgame Pandemic

Alston Raynott

ISBN: 978-988-76996-2-0 (eBook)
ISBN: 978-988-76996-3-7 (Paperback)
ISBN: 978-988-74156-8-8 (Hardcover)

Durango
New York City
Washington DC
Babeldaob
Patagonia

Prologue

In 2029, the world was brought to its knees by a pandemic unlike any other. ZIVID-29 ravaged countries across the globe, claiming millions of lives and causing widespread economic and social devastation. Governments struggled to contain the spread of the virus, implementing strict lockdowns and travel restrictions in an attempt to slow its progress. Though vaccines were eventually developed, it took years for the world to recover from the pandemic's impact.

Fast forward to 2067, and the world is a very different place. The scars left by ZIVID-29 are still visible – many cities lie in ruins, their once bustling streets now eerily quiet. Some regions have yet to fully recover from the economic fallout of the pandemic, with poverty and unemployment rampant. But the world has moved on, adapting to a new normal in which pandemics are a constant threat.

Governments around the globe have invested heavily in healthcare and disease prevention, developing new technologies and protocols to keep their citizens safe. Airports and train stations are equipped with advanced scanners that can detect signs of infection, while hospitals and clinics have been retrofitted with state-of-the-art equipment designed to handle even the most virulent diseases.

But the sense of unease in the world had been compounded by recent events. A group of mysterious extremists, fueled by a dangerous ideology, had unleashed a man-made virus unlike any seen before. The memory of ZIVID-29 – and the devastation it wrought – was still fresh in people's minds and hearts. They knew that another pandemic could strike at any moment, this time with the added threat of deliberate human intent.

It is against this backdrop that Emma and her team find themselves working tirelessly to develop a cure for the deadly new virus that has emerged seemingly out of nowhere. The stakes are higher than ever – if the virus is allowed to run rampant, its consequences could be catastrophic for the entire world.

But Emma's team is no stranger to overcoming adversity. They know what it takes to overcome seemingly insurmountable obstacles, and they are determined to do whatever it takes to find a cure for the virus. The task ahead of them is daunting, but they know that the only way to beat the virus is to work together, pooling their knowledge and expertise to crack the code and develop a cure.

In addition to their mission to develop a cure for the deadly new virus, Emma's team also realizes that they must fight against the group of extremists responsible for unleashing it upon the world. They know that finding and stopping these dangerous individuals is just as critical as developing a cure.

1

The Outbreak in Durango

Dr. Emma Lee, who is one of the top virologists in the world, sat in the back of the van, scrolling through her notes on a virus outbreak. Her team was called in to investigate a strange virus that had been spreading rapidly in Durango, a small town in the Western United States. The reports were vague, but they mentioned symptoms like fever, coughing, and fatigue.

As the van pulled up to the local hospital, Emma felt a sense of unease. The parking lot was packed with cars, and people were rushing in and out of the building. Ambulances were parked haphazardly in front of the entrance, and the sounds of sirens filled the air.

The team got out of the van and quickly donned their hazmat suits, ready to assess the situation. Dr. Daniel Li, the team's virologist and medical expert in infectious diseases, was the first to step into the hospital. Next, Dr. Laura Chen, the pathologist, and Dr. Mike Patel, the microbiologist followed Daniel's steps. Emma and the rest, Sarah Kim the expert in patient care and John Smith the security specialist, followed closely behind, taking in the scene around them.

Emma's colleagues on the team also included Dr. Maria Rodriguez, an immunologist, and Dr. Tom Johnson, an epidemiologist, who were scheduled to rejoin them very soon after completing their medical project in Japan.

The hospital was in chaos. People were coughing and vomiting in the hallways, while others lay in beds, their faces pale and their breathing shallow. Doctors and nurses were running from room to room in rapid pace, trying to keep up with the influx of patients.

Emma and her team made their way to the hospital's emergency room, where they were met by Jenny, the head nurse. She looked haggard and exhausted, but she tried to maintain a professional demeanor as she explained the situation.

"We've had a sudden influx of patients with respiratory symptoms," Jenny said. "Most of them have a fever and a cough, but some of them are having trouble breathing. We don't know what's causing it."

Emma was silent, taking notes as the nurse spoke. "Is there any pattern to the patients?" she asked.

Jenny shook her head. "Not that we can see. They're from different age groups and backgrounds. Some of them were healthy before they got sick, while others had underlying conditions. We're doing our best to treat them, but we're running out of supplies."

Emma exchanged a worried glance with Daniel. They had seen outbreaks like this before, but this one seemed different. The symptoms were severe and seemed to be affecting a wide range of people. They needed to find out what was causing it, and fast.

"Thank you," Emma said to Jenny. "We'll take it from here."

As they walked through the hospital, the team witnessed the dire impact of the virus on the healthcare system. The emergency room was overflowing with patients who were severely ill and in need of immediate medical attention. The scene was chaotic, with doctors and nurses rushing back and forth to tend to their patients, while the air was thick with the sound of coughing, wheezing, and moaning.

The team could see the exhaustion on the faces of the healthcare workers, who had been working around the clock to provide care for the sick. The hospital corridors were lined with beds, and patients were lying there, hooked up to machines, struggling to breathe. The sheer number of people affected by the virus was overwhelming and heart-wrenching, leaving the team feeling a mix of sadness and helplessness.

She turned to the fellow. "We need to get to work," she said. "Let's start with taking some samples and running tests. We need to figure out what we're dealing with."

The team understood, and they quickly got to work, taking samples from the sick patients and analyzing them in their makeshift lab. As the hours passed, they began to uncover some clues about the virus, but the more they learned, the more worried they became.

By the end of the day, they were exhausted, but they knew that they had to keep working. They had a long road ahead of them, and they were just getting started. The virus was spreading, and they had to stop it before it was too late.

2

The Possible Origin of a Mysterious Virus

Next day, as the team began to delve deeper into their investigation, they discovered that this virus was unlike any they had ever seen before. The symptoms were not only severe but also appeared to be mutating at an alarming rate. Patients who were initially stable quickly deteriorated, with their organs failing one by one, and there seemed to be no way to stop the virus from ravaging their bodies.

They discovered that the virus was airborne, making it highly contagious, and it seemed to be able to survive on surfaces for an extended period, making it difficult to contain.

Dr. Maria Rodriguez and Dr. Tom Johnson entered the hospital room, where Emma and Daniel were discussing the situation with the local doctors.

Tom spoke up, "What's going on here? Why are there so many patients in critical condition?"

Emma replied, "We're still trying to figure it out, but it seems like a virus is causing these symptoms. We suspect it's highly contagious and deadly."

Maria interjected, "But viruses usually affect specific age groups or demographics. Why is this one affecting everyone?"

Daniel added, "That's what's making this virus particularly unusual. It's indiscriminate in its victims. We're also seeing severe neurological symptoms, which is alarming."

Tom looked concerned, "What do you mean by neurological symptoms?"

Daniel explained, "The virus is attacking the nervous system, causing severe neurological symptoms that are difficult to treat. Patients are not responding to the treatments usually prescribed for similar symptoms, and their conditions are deteriorating rapidly."

Maria shook her head in disbelief, "This is really concerning. We need to act fast and figure out how to contain this virus before it spreads any further."

As the team continued their investigation, they found that the virus was mutating rapidly, making it difficult to find a cure. In addition to its high contagion rate and neurological effects, the virus seemed to be resistant to most antiviral medications, making it challenging to treat. The team was running out of options and knew that they needed to find a cure quickly if they were to save any lives.

The strange virus had the potential to become a global health crisis if left unchecked, and the team knew that they were up against a formidable foe. With each passing moment, the virus was spreading, and more lives were at risk. The stakes were high, and failure was not an option.

Daniel, who was leading the team's medical investigations, looked at the test results and shook his head in disbelief. "Sigh, I'm 100% sure now this virus is highly infectious and deadly," he said, his voice grave. "It's unlike anything we've ever seen before."

Emma's heart sank. She knew that if they didn't act quickly, the virus could spread beyond the small town and turn into a full-blown pandemic. "We need to find out where it came from," she said, her voice firm. "We can't afford to waste any time."

As the team continued their investigations, they found evidence that suggested that the virus may not have been a natural occurrence. They discovered that several of the patients had recently traveled to a foreign country and had close contact with animals while there. Emma's mind immediately went to the possibility of a bioterrorism attack.

"We need to consider the possibility that this outbreak may have been deliberate," she said, her voice urgent. "We need to look into the backgrounds of the patients and see if there's a connection to any extremist groups or individuals who may have an agenda against our country."

Daniel nodded in agreement. "We'll look into any possible connections," he said.

As the team dug deeper into the investigation, they found more evidence to support their theory. They discovered that several patients had received anonymous packages containing mysterious powders and liquids, which they had ingested, thinking they were natural remedies. The team immediately suspected that someone might use the virus as a weapon.

"We need to notify the WHO (World Health Organization) and other relevant agencies immediately," Sarah said, her voice resolute. "We can't handle this outbreak alone." Emma's phone rang. This was a bad call from the WHO. Another outbreak, and this time in New York City with over 80,000 patients in just one week. She knew what this meant. Her team would have to drop everything and go there for another urgent investigation.

Emma quickly broke the news to them. The team members were shocked and saddened to hear about the scale of the outbreak. However, they knew they had to act fast, as time was of the essence in situations like these. The team immediately started making arrangements to leave for

NYC. They packed their bags and took a flight to NYC in the next morning.

3

Alarming Discoveries

Upon their arrival in NYC, the team was greeted by a chaotic scene. The hospitals were overflowing with patients, and the medical staff were struggling to keep up with the demand for treatment.

They decided to interview patients and collected samples from the NYC Medical Hospital+, the largest hospital in NYC.

The team spent the next few hours interviewing patients and their families. They gathered information about their medical histories, recent travels, and any other relevant details that could help them understand the outbreak. As they moved from one room to another, they noticed some unusual symptoms and patterns that they could not explain.

In one room, they met with a young boy Nick who had been admitted to the hospital with a high fever and severe cough. Michelle, his mother, who was sitting next to him, looked exhausted and worried. Emma introduced herself and her team and asked the mother about Nick's symptoms.

"He's been coughing non-stop for the past two days, and his fever won't go down," the mother said. "We thought it was just a cold, but then he started having trouble breathing, and we had to rush him here."

As Laura and Mike examined the boy, she noticed that he had small red spots on his skin. She asked Michelle if Nick had a rash, but she shook her head.

"No, he didn't have a rash before. These spots appeared just a few hours ago," the mother said worriedly, pointing to the red spots.

Sarah made a note of the new symptom and moved on to the next room. In the next room, they met with Eleanor, an elderly woman who had been admitted to the hospital with a headache and confusion. Eleanor's daughter Karen, who was by her side, explained that her mother had been acting strangely for the past few days.

"She's been forgetting things, and she's been having trouble speaking," Karen said. "She's always been sharp and quick-witted, but now she seems confused and disoriented."

Laura listened carefully and asked the daughter if her mother had any other symptoms. The daughter mentioned that her mother had also been experiencing muscle weakness and tremors.

As the team continued their interviews, they started to notice some unusual patterns. The virus seemed to be affecting people of all ages and backgrounds, just like in Durango. But now they were seeing new symptoms that were not typical of respiratory infections.

After they finished interviewing all the patients and their families, the team members gathered in a conference room on the top floor of the NYC Medical Hospital+ to discuss their findings.

"Did anyone else notice the red spots on Nick's skin?" Emma asked, looking at her team.

"Yes, I saw them too," Maria replied. "I've never seen anything like that before."

"And the confusion and muscle weakness in the elderly woman?" Tom added. "Those are neurological symptoms, which is not typical of a respiratory virus."

Emma nodded. "Exactly. We need to investigate this further. We should also contact the WHO and ask for their assistance."

"But what if it's a new virus that we don't have a cure for?" Mike asked.

"We'll cross that bridge when we get there," Emma replied. "Right now, we need to gather as much information as we can and work with the WHO to contain the outbreak."

4

A Violent Attack

The team moved to the NYC Medical Research Center and continued their work in a research facility full of hunched over microscopes, pipettes, test tubes, computers, and tablets.

They had barely settled into their quarters when the alarm sounded at 9:00 pm. Emma bolted upright, her heart pounding as she recognized the emergency signal. She quickly dressed in her thermal gear and rushed to the makeshift lab, where the others were already gathering.

"What's happening?" Emma asked, trying to catch her breath.

"Laura was attacked," John said, his face pale.

Emma felt a cold knot form in her stomach. Laura was one of their most valuable members, an expert in pathology and a key player in their mission. If she was hurt or worse, it would be a major blow to their efforts.

"Where is she?" Emma asked, her voice tense.

"In the greenhouse, the right-hand side of the main building," Mike replied.

As Emma headed towards the door, her mind was already racing. The greenhouse was a large, domed structure that housed their research on plant-based treatments for the virus. It was also one of the most vulnerable areas in the facility, with large windows and few defenses.

As Emma sprinted down the corridor, she heard shouts and screams from ahead. She skidded around a corner and saw a group of people with masks and weapons attacking the greenhouse. They were throwing rocks and bottles, smashing the windows and trying to force their way inside.

Emma's heart sank as she recognized the attackers. They were the same group of rioters who had been protesting outside the WHO headquarters in Geneva, claiming that the outbreak was a government conspiracy. Emma had dismissed them as cranks, but now it seemed they were willing to use violence to achieve their goals.

Emma drew her own weapon and ran towards the group, shouting for them to stop. But they ignored her, intent on their mission. Emma saw Laura inside, huddled behind a table, her face bruised and bloody. Emma's blood boiled with anger as she saw her colleague being attacked.

"Stop!" Emma shouted, her voice echoing through the greenhouse. "This is a research facility. You have no right to be here!"

The attackers turned to face her, their weapons raised. Emma could see the hatred in their eyes, the conviction that they were doing the right thing. She tried to reason with them, to explain that they were all on the same side, fighting against the virus. But they wouldn't listen.

"She works for the government. Kill her! Kill her!" One of the rioters loudly shouted and several rioters then turned and walked towards her.

Emma's training kicked in as she fired her weapon, aiming for the ground near the attackers' feet. The sound was deafening in the confined space, and the attackers flinched back. Emma used the distraction to rush towards Laura, grabbing her arm and pulling her towards the door.

The attackers followed them, throwing more rocks and bottles. Emma fired her weapon again, this time hitting one of the attackers in the shoulder. He cried out in pain, but his comrades only redoubled their efforts.

Emma and Laura made it to the door, but the attackers were right behind them. Emma fired her weapon one last time, hitting the door controls and sealing it shut. She could hear the attackers pounding on the door, but she knew it wouldn't hold for long.

"We have to get out of here," Emma said, her voice urgent.

Laura nodded, and they ran towards the nearest exit. As they burst out into the cold air, Emma saw that the attackers had also breached the main lab. Smoke and flames billowed out of the building, and Emma knew that their mission was in jeopardy.

"We have to stop them," Emma said, determination in her voice. "We can't let them destroy everything we've worked for."

With a determined look on her face, Laura agreed to join the fight. She knew that it was going to be dangerous, but she wasn't going to back down now. Emma felt her heart racing with adrenaline as they charged towards the lab, fully geared up and ready for battle.

As they approached the group of attackers, Laura's grim expression didn't waver. They knew what they had to do – take down the enemy at all costs. Without hesitation, they took a deep breath and charged forward, firing their weapons in the air.

The sound of gunfire echoed through the air as the attackers turned to face them, but Emma and Laura didn't flinch. They continued to fire and shout, driving the attackers back towards the door. The enemies were no match for Emma and Laura's unwavering courage and strength.

With each shot fired, the attackers retreated, dropping their weapons and fleeing into the darkness. Emma and Laura stood their ground until the last of the attackers disappeared into the night. The two women were exhausted but triumphant, knowing that they had just won a hard-fought victory against all odds. Their hearts still racing with excitement, they shared a victorious smile, proud of their bravery and unbreakable bond.

5

Is the Virus Engineered?

Through this entire night of the rioters' torment, the team just took a break of several hours and they continued to work tirelessly through the night, analyzing the samples they had collected from the infected patients.

Emma was examining a slide under the microscope when she noticed unusual something. The virus particles were arranged in a peculiar pattern that she had never seen before. She called over Mike to take a look.

"Have you seen anything like this before?" Emma asked, pointing to the slide.

Mike shook his head. "No, this is very strange. It looks like the virus has been artificially arranged in a particular pattern."

Emma nodded, deep in thought. "That's what I was thinking too. I suspect this virus may have been engineered in a lab…"

The rest of the team gathered around Emma and Mike, looking at the slide with concern. Laura, who had just returned from another medical lab, joined the group and asked, "What's going on?"

Mike explained the theory, and the team started discussing the implications of their discovery. If the virus had been engineered, it could mean that it was released intentionally, possibly as a bioweapon.

Maria, the team's immunologist, spoke up. "We need to do more tests to confirm our suspicions. We should compare the virus samples with other known viruses and see if we can identify any similarities or differences."

"That's a good idea. Let's get started on that right away. Mike, can you prepare the samples for sequencing?" Emma said.

Mike nodded and headed to the lab bench to start the process. The rest of the team continued their analysis of the virus samples, discussing the possible implications of their discovery.

As they worked, Emma couldn't shake the feeling of unease that had settled in the pit of her stomach. If the virus had been engineered, who had created it? And why?

The team worked through the night, taking turns resting and analyzing the samples. As the sun rose over NYC, they finally had some answers. The sequencing results confirmed their suspicions – the virus had indeed been engineered in a lab.

The team was shocked and frightened by this discovery. It meant that the outbreak was not a natural occurrence but had been deliberately created and released. They had to act quickly to stop the spread of the virus and find a cure.

Emma gathered the team together for an urgent meeting, knowing that they had to share their recent findings. As they sat down around the table, Emma took a deep breath and began to speak.

"Team, we have made a discovery that changes everything. We believed that this virus was not a natural occurrence – it was intentionally created by someone with ill intentions. We must now operate under the assumption that this person or group had a specific target in mind, and it is our responsibility to find out who that is."

The room fell silent as everyone absorbed the magnitude of Emma's words. Maria was the first to speak up, her voice laced with concern. "We also need to determine how the virus was released and what measures we can take to prevent it from happening again."

Sarah chimed in, agreeing with Maria's sentiment. "That's a good point. We need to investigate every possibility and gather as much information as we can. Our priority should be to contain the outbreak and minimize its impact on society while finding those responsible for unleashing this deadly virus."

The team dispersed to begin their investigation, each member taking on a different task. Emma sat down at her desk and began reviewing the data they had collected so far. As she analyzed the information, she realized that the virus was evolving at an alarming rate. If they didn't find a cure soon, it could mutate into an even deadlier form.

6

A Terrifying Threat

The message on the computer screen was chilling. The team stared at it, wide-eyed and silent.

"We know who you are. We know what you're doing. Leave town now or face the consequences."

Emma took a deep breath and tried to steady herself. She had known this was a possibility from the moment they arrived in New York City. But seeing the words on the screen, the threat so real and immediate, made it all too terrifying.

She turned to her team, who were still staring at the message in disbelief. "We need to take this seriously," she said, her voice firm. "Everyone, lock down the facility. We need to make sure we're secure before we do anything else."

John quickly sprang into action, following Emma's orders without question. He secured all the entrances and exits of the research facility, locking them down with heavy steel doors and electronic security systems. They checked the windows, making sure they were all locked and sealed tight.

Once the facility was secure, Emma turned her attention back to the message on the screen. She had a feeling she knew who it was from.

"Did we get a trace on the message?" she asked her team.

"Yes, I managed to trace the IP address. It's coming from a local coffee shop, about a few miles from here," Mike said.

"Okay, we need to investigate. But we can't just barge in there. We need to be careful." Emma said and she looked at them.

"Who's up for a little reconnaissance mission?" Emma asked.

There were murmurs of assent from the team, and Emma felt a surge of pride. They were a good group, and they were all committed to finding out the truth.

"Okay, okay," she said, clapping her hands together. "Let's get ready. We're going to need some disguises."

They arrived at the coffee shop an hour later, dressed in casual clothes and wearing hats and sunglasses. Emma's heart was pounding as they entered the shop, scanning the faces of the patrons for any sign of the extremists.

The coffee shop was busy, and Emma felt a jolt of fear as she realized how many people could be involved. But she pushed the thought aside and focused on the task at hand.

They split up into groups, each taking a different section of the shop to investigate. Emma and John approached the counter, ordering a coffee and scanning the faces of the employees.

There was a man behind the counter, his face friendly but guarded. John felt a prickle of suspicion and tried to get a closer look at his name tag. But before he could, there was a commotion at the back of the shop.

Emma spun around, her hand going to the gun at her waist. But it was Laura waving her over.

"Emma, you need to see this," she said, her voice urgent.

Emma followed Laura to the back of the shop, where a group of men were huddled around a tablet. She took a step closer, her eyes fixed on the tablet. On the screen was a video, playing on a loop. It showed footage of the infected patients from the research facility, writhing in agony as they were consumed by the virus. Emma's heart sank as she watched, the images filling her with a sense of dread and despair.

"What do they want?" Emma turned to Laura and sked, her voice barely above a whisper.

"They want us to back off," Laura replied, her eyes scanning the message again. "They say that the outbreak is a government conspiracy, and they won't let us interfere with their plans."

Emma's mind raced as she tried to make sense of the situation. Who were these people, and what did they hope to achieve by unleashing a deadly virus on innocent people? She knew that she had to find out, and quickly.

"Get the team on this," Emma said, her voice firm. "I want to know who sent this message and where it came from. We need to track these people down before they can do any more damage."

Laura understood, already reaching for her smart phone. "I'll get right on it," she said, her eyes focused on the screen. "In the meantime, we need to make sure that everyone on the team is safe. We can't take any chances with these people."

Emma agreed, her mind already racing with ideas. She knew that they were in a race against time, and that the fate of humanity was at stake.

"Get the team together," Emma said, her voice firm. "We need to come up with a plan, and fast. We can't let these people get away with this."

Laura nodded, her eyes filled with determination. "We won't," she said. "We'll stop them, no matter what it takes."

Emma felt a surge of confidence as she watched Laura walk out of the coffee shop, her steps quick and purposeful. She knew that they might have a long road ahead of them, filled with danger and uncertainty. But she also knew that they had the skills and determination to see it through.

7

A Visit to the Innovatech Research Institute

Emma, Daniel, Maria and Tom were on the move again. They had followed a lead that took them to a nearby research facility, called the Innovatech Research Institute. Emma had a feeling that this might be their best chance yet to uncover the truth behind the outbreak. She hoped that they would find some answers here.

As they approached the facility, they were stopped by a group of armed guards. The guards demanded to know what they were doing there.

"We're from the WHO," Emma said, holding up her identification badge. "We're here to investigate the outbreak and we need to speak to the scientists in charge."

The guards looked at each other for a moment before one of them spoke up. "You're not authorized to be here. You need to leave now."

Emma was taken aback. She had expected some resistance, but she had hoped that their badges would be enough to get them in.

"We need to speak to someone in charge," she repeated, trying to keep her tone calm.

"I'm sorry," the guard said, "but I can't let you in."

Emma could feel her frustration building. She didn't have time for this. They needed answers and they needed them now. "Listen," she said firmly, "we're here to help. We're not leaving until we get some answers."

The guard looked at her for a moment before sighing. "Fine," he said, "I'll see what I can do."

A guard disappeared into the facility and Emma and her team waited anxiously outside. After a few minutes, he returned with a woman in a lab coat. "This is Danielnda Black," he said, "she's in charge of the research institute."

Dr. Black looked at Emma and her fellow with suspicion. "What do you want?" she asked.

"We're investigating the outbreak," Daniel said, "and we need your help. We think that this virus may have been engineered in a lab and we need to know if your facility had anything to do with it."

Dr. Black's expression hardened. "I can assure you that our facility had nothing to do with this outbreak," she said, her voice cold.

"We just need to ask you a few questions," Tom said, trying to keep his tone friendly. "We're not here to cause any trouble."

Dr. Black sighed. "Fine," she said, "come with me."

She led them into the facility and down a long hallway. As they walked, Emma couldn't help but feel like they were being watched. She glanced around, trying to see if there were any cameras, but she didn't see anything.

Finally, they reached a large room filled with scientists, lab equipment and powerful quantum computers. Daniel could feel his excitement growing. Maybe they would finally find some answers here.

Dr. Black gestured for them to take a seat at a nearby table. "What do you want to know?" she asked, her tone impatient.

"We're interested in any research you've done on viruses," Maria said. "Specifically, we want to know if you've worked on anything similar to the virus that's causing this outbreak."

Dr. Black hesitated for a moment before answering. "We've worked on a lot of viruses," she said. "I'll need to check our records to see if we've worked on anything that matches the description you're giving me."

Emma assented. "That's a start," she said.

Dr. Black disappeared into another room and they waited anxiously. After fifteen minutes, she returned with a file in her hand. "We did work on a virus that shares some similarities with the one that's causing this outbreak," she said, handing the file to Maria and Tom.

Maria quickly flipped through the pages, scanning the information. "This is helpful," she said.

Dr. Black nodded. "I'm glad we could assist you. But I must remind you that we have protocols to follow, and we cannot allow you to take any of these documents outside of this facility."

Tom sighed. "We understand, but we're dealing with a potentially dangerous virus here. Lives are at stake. Can't you see that?"

Dr. Black's expression softened. "Believe me, I understand the severity of the situation. But we have our own procedures to follow. I can try to get authorization for you to access more information, but it will take some time."

Emma nodded. "We'll need to set up a secure communication channel so we can stay in touch."

Dr. Black agreed. "I'll arrange for a secure line to be established. In the meantime, I can show you around the facility and answer any questions you may have."

As they made their way through the facility, the team was surprised by how advanced the technology was. They saw rows of lab equipment, computer servers, and medical devices. They also noticed that the facility had multiple levels, each with restricted access.

"Wow, this is impressive," said Emma and Daniel, as they entered a room filled with high-tech machinery. "What kind of research is being conducted here?"

Dr. Black hesitated for a moment before answering. "Um…, I'm afraid I can't reveal too much about our current projects, but we mainly focus on genetic research and disease control."

Maria raised an eyebrow. "Interesting. And what about the virus we're dealing with? Do you have any information that could help us?"

Dr. Black hesitated again before speaking. "I'm sorry, but I'm not at liberty to disclose any information about that particular virus. We have strict confidentiality agreements in place with our clients."

Daniel and Tom frowned together. "Clients? Who are your clients?"

Dr. Black's face grew tense. "I'm sorry, I cannot discuss that with you."

Emma and her team exchanged a worried look. It was clear that they were not going to get any more information out of Dr. Black.

"Thank you for your help, Dr. Black," said Emma, as they prepared to leave the facility. "We'll be in touch if we need anything else."

Dr. Black nodded reluctantly. "Please be careful. I hope you find what you're looking for." As they made their way back to the car, the team discussed the findings.

"That was a dead end," Maria said. "We didn't get anything useful out of them."

Emma shook her head. "Not entirely. Did you notice how secretive they were being? It's clear they're hiding something. We need to dig deeper and find out what that is."

"I agree," said Tom. "But how do we do that? They're not going to give us any more information willingly."

Emma thought for a moment. "We need to find a way to access their confidential data. If we can hack into their system, we might be able to uncover some useful information."

"That's a risky move, but it might be our only option," Daniel said.

Emma looked at them with determination. "We're going to do whatever it takes to stop this virus from spreading. Even if it means taking some risks."

With that, they got back into the car and drove off, ready to tackle the next challenge that lay ahead.

8

The PathogenX Laboratory

Emma and her team had managed to obtain some useful information from the scientists at the Innovatech Research Institute, but they knew that they needed more concrete evidence to confirm their suspicions. They decided to sneak into the facility at night and search for anything that could help them uncover the truth.

As they approached the institute, they could see that it was heavily guarded, with armed personnel patrolling the perimeter. They split up into three groups, each group taking a different route to avoid detection. They had to move quickly and quietly, staying out of sight and avoiding any tripwires or alarms.

After several minutes of sneaking around, Maria, Mike and Sarah stumbled upon a room in the restricted area. It was called "PathogenX Laboratory" that seemed to be some sort of lab. They cautiously pushed the door open and peered inside, their eyes widening in shock at what she saw.

The lab was filled with cages containing animals of all kinds, from rats to monkeys. The animals looked sick and weak, and some were convulsing violently. Tubes and wires ran from the cages to machines that were beeping and flashing with alarming frequency.

Maria felt sick to her stomach as she believed that these animals were being used for experimentation, likely to test the virus they had been studying. She knew that this was unethical and inhumane, and she felt a deep anger and sadness at the sight.

"Guys, you need to see this," she said, using her radio to call the rest of the team. "I think we've found the evidence we were looking for."

The team quickly regrouped and entered PathogenX Lab. They carefully searched through the paperwork and data files, taking photos and making notes. They found some research papers and presentations detailing the genetic engineering techniques, such as CRISPR-Cas9, to create "Virocide X", the name of the virus. In fact, the process involves manipulating the genetic material, DNA or RNA, of a virus to change its characteristics or behavior to make it more infectious, more lethal, or more resistant to treatments or vaccines. They also found evidence that the virus had been deliberately released into the population.

"Virocide X, we found you!" Sarah spoke in a low and deep voice.

"I can't believe it. It sounds terrible…," Emma said.

As they were finishing up their search, they heard the sound of approaching footsteps. Emma quickly whispered to the team to hide, and they ducked behind some of the cages. A group of armed guards entered the lab, looking tense and alert.

"We've got intruders," one of them shouted, his gun pointed at the team. "Identify yourselves and come out with your hands up."

The team knew that they had been caught, and that they were in serious danger. They slowly emerged from their hiding spots, their hands raised in surrender.

"Easy! Easy! Men, we're scientists, we're just scientists" Emma said, trying to sound as convincing as possible. "We were sent here to investigate the outbreak and find a cure."

The guards looked skeptical, but they didn't immediately open fire. Instead, they ordered the team to follow them, leading them at gunpoint to a nearby room. Once inside, the team was ordered to sit on the ground, their hands still raised. Emma could feel her heart pounding in her chest as she tried to come up with a plan. She knew that they needed to escape, and fast.

Suddenly, one of the guards' radios crackled to life. The team could hear a voice on the other end, speaking urgently.

"We've got reports of a riot in town," the voice said. "All available personnel need to head back immediately. Repeat, all available personnel need to head back immediately."

The guards hesitated for a moment, exchanging glances. Then, one of them spoke up.

"Looks like we've got bigger problems than a few scientists," he said, lowering his gun. "You guys are lucky. We'll let you go this time, but if we catch you snooping around again, we won't be so lenient."

The team breathed a sigh of relief as they were released. They quickly made their way out of the facility, back to their van. Emma was still reeling from the shock of what they had discovered, but she knew that they were one step closer to uncovering the truth behind the outbreak.

As they drove back to the research facility, they couldn't help but feel a sense of relief wash over them. They had accomplished what they set out to do, but the weight of their discovery hung heavy in the air.

Once they were back in their makeshift lab, Emma gathered her team together for a debriefing. They sat around a small table, sipping on lukewarm coffee as they discussed what they had found.

"So, what's our next move?" asked Maria, looking around the group.

Tom leaned back in his chair and rubbed his temples, deep in thought. "We need to get this information to the right people," he said. "We can't keep this to ourselves."

"But who do we trust?" asked Laura, her eyes narrowed in suspicion. "We don't know who's involved in this conspiracy."

Emma sighed heavily. She knew that Laura had a point. It was a risky move to go to the authorities without knowing who was involved in the conspiracy, but they couldn't just sit on the information they had uncovered.

"We'll have to be careful," she said. "We'll need to find someone who we can trust and who has the authority to investigate this."

The team said nothing, but the tension in the room was palpable. They all knew that they were in dangerous territory, and that their lives could be at risk. When they continued to discuss their next steps, Emma's smart phone buzzed on the table. She picked it up and saw that she had a new message. It was from an unknown number.

"Guys, we have a problem," she said, showing the message to her team.

The message read, **"I know what you're up to. Stay out of this if you value your lives."**

The team exchanged worried glances, and Emma felt a knot form in her stomach. They had known that they were taking a risk by investigating the outbreak, but she hadn't anticipated just how dangerous it could be.

After a while of silence.

"This is a threat again, but we can't back down now," Mike said firmly. "We need to see this through." Others agreed, but Emma could tell that they were all feeling the weight of the situation. They were in too deep to turn back now.

As the night wore on, Emma sat alone in her resting room, staring at the ceiling as she tried to process everything that had happened. She knew that she needed to get some rest, but sleep felt impossible.

She was startled by a knock on the door, and she quickly got to her feet, her heart racing. She cautiously made her way over to the door and looked through the peephole. It was Tom.

"Can I come in?" he asked, looking pale and shaken. Emma said yes, and he stepped inside. "What's wrong?" she asked, closing the door behind him.

He took a deep breath and looked at her with haunted eyes. "I just got a call from my wife," he said. "She's been infected."

Emma felt the air rush out of her lungs. She knew that this was a possibility, but it still felt like a devastating blow.

"We need to get her help," she said, her mind racing. "We'll find a way to get her treatment."

Tom agreed, but Emma could see the fear and despair etched on his face. They were all in this together, but the personal toll of their mission was starting to weigh heavily on them.

As the night continued to wear on, Emma sat with Tom, trying to come up with a plan. They couldn't let their emotions cloud their judgement, but it was becoming increasingly difficult to keep their cool. They knew that they were up against a mysterious and dangerous enemy, but they also knew that they couldn't back down.

Emma said, "We need to keep pushing forward. We have to find out who is responsible for this and stop them before it's too late." She pulled out her laptop and began to sort through the files and documents they had obtained from the research facility. As she read through the information, a sense of dread washed over her. It was clear that Virocide X had been deliberately engineered, but the purpose behind it was still unclear. She needed more information, and fast.

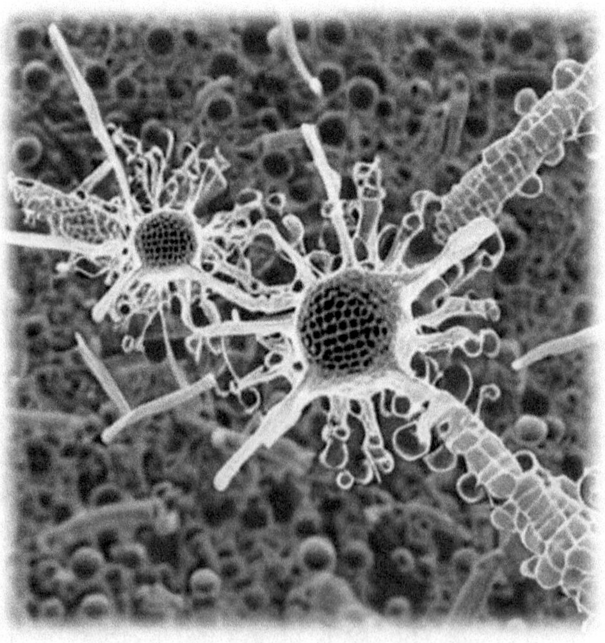

9

Chaos and Danger at the NYC Medical Hospital+

They returned to the NYC Medical Hospital+ for collecting more samples. As they drove towards the hospital, the team could sense the tension in the air. The streets were more crowded than before, with people rushing around frantically. They could hear the sound of sirens in the distance, and the occasional scream or shout pierced through the noise.

When they arrived at the hospital, they found it surrounded by police and military vehicles, with armed guards stationed at the entrance. Emma approached one of the guards and showed her ID.

"We're from the WHO. We were here a few days ago," she said. "We need to collect some samples and talk to the doctors again."

The guard eyed her suspiciously. "I don't know," he said. "Things are pretty crazy in there. It's not safe."

"We're trained professionals," John said. "We know how to handle ourselves. Please, let us through."

After some more persuasion, the guard finally relented and let them in. As they made their way through the hospital, they saw more evidence of the chaos that had ensued. Patients were lying in the hallways, moaning and writhing in pain. Doctors and nurses rushed back and forth, their faces grim and tired.

They made their way to the wing where they had collected samples before. They were greeted by Dr. Jordan, who looked exhausted but relieved to see them.

"Thank god you're here," she said. "Things have gotten so much worse. We've had more cases in the past few hours than we've had in the past week."

Maria nodded grimly. "We need to collect more samples," she said. "And we need to talk to anyone who might have information about how this outbreak started."

Dr. Jordan led them to a makeshift lab, where they began collecting samples and analyzing them. As they worked, they could hear the sound of screaming and shouting coming from outside.

"What's going on out there?" Sarah asked.

"It's the infected," Dr. Jordan said. "Some of them have become violent. They're attacking anyone they come across."

Sarah felt a knot form in her stomach. This was worse than she had feared. They needed to find a way to stop the spread of the virus before it was too late.

As they worked, they were interrupted by a commotion outside. They could hear the sound of glass breaking and people shouting. They rushed to the door and looked out into the hallway immediately.

They saw a group of infected patients, their eyes wild and their movements erratic, attacking a group of guards. The guards were yelling at them and struggling to hold them off, firing their guns and swinging their batons. But there were too many of the infected, and they seemed to be getting stronger by the minute.

The team knew they had to do something. John turned to Dr. Jordan. "We need to get out of here," he said. "But we can't leave these people behind. We have to find a way to help them."

Dr. Jordan agreed, her face grim. "I'll see if I can find some sedatives," she said. "Maybe we can calm them down enough to get them out of here."

The team worked quickly, gathering supplies and preparing to make a run for it. They could hear the sounds of gunfire and screaming growing louder by the minute. As they made their way towards the exit, they encountered more infected patients, their red eyes fixed on them hungrily. Tom, Mike and John fought them off as best they could, using whatever weapons they could find.

Finally, they reached the exit, where they were met by another group of guards. The guards looked relieved to see them, but also wary.

"What's going on in there?" Michael, who is one of the guards, asked.

"It's bad, extremely bad" Daniel wheezed. "We need to get out of here before it's too late."

But before they could leave, they heard a loud commotion from the direction of the emergency room. Shouts and screams echoed through the halls.

They rushed towards the noise, their hearts pounding with fear. When they arrived at the ER, they found a chaotic scene. Patients were thrashing and screaming, their red eyes wild with fever. Nurses and doctors were struggling to hold them down and administer medication.

"What's going on here?" Emma demanded, pushing her way through the crowd.

One of the nurses turned to her, her face pale with fear. "We don't know. We don't know," she said hysterically. "These patients just started getting worse. They're delirious and violent."

John and Maria surveyed the scene, trying to make sense of it all. Something was definitely different about these patients. They seemed more agitated, more out of control.

"Get out of here!" one of the doctors shouted. "It's not safe!" But the team didn't budge. They had a job to do, and they weren't going to abandon it now.

"We need to take some samples," Tom insisted, pulling on a pair of gloves. "Find out what's going on with these patients."

The team worked quickly and efficiently, collecting samples from the infected patients. But as they worked, they couldn't shake the feeling that something was watching them.

Emma looked up to see a group of men standing in the doorway, watching them with cold, calculating eyes. She recognized them immediately as the same extremists who had attacked Laura.

"What are you doing here?" Emma demanded, her voice shaking with anger.

The leader of the group stepped forward, a cruel smile on his face. "We're here to put an end to this so-called investigation," he said. "We know the truth. This outbreak was caused by your government, and we won't rest until justice is served."

Emma's blood ran cold. These men were dangerous, and they wouldn't hesitate to hurt anyone who got in their way.

"Get out of here," she said, her voice low and steady. "Before things get ugly."

The men hesitated for a moment, as if considering their options. But then they turned and left, disappearing back into the chaos of the hospital.

10

Endless Firefights

Emma and the fellows rushed out of the hospital, running towards their car. They knew they had to leave before the situation got any worse. But before they could reach their vehicle, they heard a group of people shouting behind them. John turned around and saw a group of masked individuals, wielding guns and baseball bats, running towards them.

"Get down!" John yelled as he pulled out his gun and took cover behind a nearby car. Others followed suit, taking cover and drawing their weapons.

The sound of gunshots echoed through the air as the two groups exchanged fire. The team was outnumbered, but John was very well-trained and determined to fight back. John guided the members to fire their weapons with precision, aiming for the gunmen's legs and arms in an attempt to disarm them.

The fight was intense and chaotic, with bullets whizzing by and car windows shattering. Emma could feel her heart pounding in her chest as she ducked behind the car, trying to avoid the hail of bullets.

"We need to get out of here!" Daniel and Sarah shouted simultaneously. Other members agreed and they couldn't stay there any longer. They needed to get to safety and regroup.

"Covering fire!" John yelled as he peeked out from behind the car and fired off a few shots. The team followed his lead, providing covering fire as they retreated towards their car.

The extremists were relentless, firing at them as they tried to escape. But the team was determined and kept moving forward, taking out as many of their attackers as possible.

Finally, they reached their car and piled inside. Daniel slammed the door shut and started the engine, speeding away from the scene of the ambush. They could hear the sound of gunfire fading away as they drove further and further from danger.

As they drove, all of them couldn't help but feel shaken by the ambush. It was clear that the extremists were organized and well-equipped. They couldn't take them lightly.

"Guys, we need to be more careful from now on," Laura said, her voice serious. They knew that they were probably up against a dangerous enemy, and they needed to be prepared for whatever came their way. The drive to a hotel was tense and quiet, with everyone lost in their own thoughts. They had narrowly escaped a potentially deadly situation, and the reality of their situation was starting to sink in.

When they finally arrived at a hotel several miles away from the hospital, all members quickly made their way to their rooms. Indeed, they needed to rest and regroup, to figure out their next move.

As Emma lay in bed, staring up at the ceiling, she knew that they had a long and difficult road ahead of them. But she was determined to see this through, to uncover the truth behind the outbreak and bring those responsible to justice. No matter what it took.

After taking a few hours of rest, the team retrieved their car in tense silence. Suddenly, sound of gunshots broke the tense silence, causing Emma and the team to dive for cover behind a nearby parked car. They peered around the edge of the vehicle, trying to identify their attackers. In the distance, they could see a group of men clad in black, armed with assault rifles and moving towards them.

"We've got company," Emma whispered, her heart pounding in her chest. "Be ready for anything." They scrambled to get their own weapons ready, checking their ammunition and making sure everything was in working order.

"John, take a look around," Emma ordered. John took a deep breath, trying to calm his nerves as he surveyed the area. They were surrounded on all sides, with no clear escape route.

The sound of more gunfire echoed through the air, and Maria spotted movement to her left. One of the extremists was advancing towards them, his gun at the ready. Maria raised her own weapon and fired, the recoil jolting through her arms as she took down the attacker.

More gunfire erupted, and the team shouting as they engaged in a fierce firefight. They fired round after round, taking out as many of the attackers as they could, but they seemed to be coming from all directions.

Suddenly, a voice shouted out from behind them. "Laura, get down now!"

Laura dropped to the ground, rolling to avoid the spray of bullets as a group of soldiers appeared on the scene. They were dressed in military gear and carried heavy weapons, their presence shifting the tide of the battle in their favor.

The extremists started to retreat, firing back as they ran. The team hunkered down behind the car, waiting for the shooting to stop. When the last echoes of gunfire died away, they cautiously emerged from cover, scanning the area for any remaining threats.

The soldiers approached them, their faces grim. "Are you all okay?" one of them asked.

Emma nodded, still trying to catch her breath. "Thanks to you."

The soldier shook his head. "This isn't over yet. Those extremists won't stop until they get what they want."

"What do they want?" Emma asked.

The soldier hesitated, glancing around as if checking for eavesdroppers. "We think they're after something at the hospital. Something important." Maria's mind raced as she tried to make sense of this new information. "We were just there. What could they possibly want?"

The soldier shrugged. "We don't know, but we can't let them get it. We'll take care of them from here. You need to get out of town. It's not safe."

Emma agreed, realizing the gravity of the situation. They had been thrust into the middle of a deadly game of cat and mouse, with no clear end in sight.

As they made their way back to their hotel, Emma could feel her nerves fraying. The thought of leaving New York City felt like defeat, but she knew that they had no choice. They needed to regroup and come up with a new plan of action.

As they packed up their equipment, Emma's smart phone buzzed. She glanced at the screen, seeing an unknown number.

"Hello?"

"Dr. Lee, it's Dr. Marberg."

Emma felt a surge of relief at the sound of her colleague's voice. "Dr. Marberg, are you okay?"

"I'm fine, thanks to you and your team," Dr. Marberg said. "Listen, I know you are working in NYC right now and I have some information that you need to hear. Can you meet me at the diner on Main Street?"

Emma hesitated, but she knew that they couldn't afford to ignore any leads. "Dr. Johnson, Dr. Li, Mr. Smith and I will be there at 7:00 pm."

As they made their way to the diner, Emma's mind was racing. She couldn't help but wonder what Dr. Marberg had discovered, and what it would mean for their investigation the team made it to the diner, and Emma immediately called Dr. Marberg to ask about her findings.

"Dr. Marberg, it's Emma. Have you found anything new?" she asked.

"Yes, I have," Dr. Marberg said. "As you may suspect, the virus is unlike anything we've seen before. It's highly contagious and deadly. And it was definitely engineered in a lab."

Emma's heart sank. "Are you sure?" she asked.

"Positive. Absolutely positive," Dr. Marberg said. "I've been analyzing the samples you collected, and the genetic sequence doesn't match anything in any known database.

Whoever made this virus knew exactly what they were doing."

Emma sighed. "That's not good news," she said.

"No, it's not," Dr. Marberg said. "But I've also found something else. Something that might help us stop this outbreak."

"What is it?" Tom interrupted.

"There's a specific protein that the virus targets in the human body," Dr. Marberg said. "If we can develop a drug that blocks that protein, we might be able to slow the spread of the virus and buy ourselves some time."

"That's good news," Tom said, feeling a glimmer of hope. "But it's going to take time," Dr. Marberg said. "We need to do more research and testing to develop the drug. And we need to do it fast."

Emma assented. "We'll do everything we can," she said. "Thank you, Dr. Marberg."

Abruptly, gunfire sounded outside of the diner. The team hid behind a table at once and they knew nothing but the extremists. They had to deal with the extremists and they realized that they were in for a fight, without another option.

In the twinkling of an eye, Emma, Tom, Daniel and John settled into their positions, their weapons at the ready. They could hear the sound of cars approaching in the distance, and they knew that the extremists were getting closer.

Emma's heart raced as she waited for the attackers to arrive. A second later, the sound of gunfire filled the air as the extremists launched their attack. They fought back fiercely, taking cover behind tables and counters, firing their weapons at the attackers.

The battle was intense and brutal, with no clear advantage for either side. Emma could feel the adrenaline pumping through her veins as she fired her gun, trying to take down as many of the attackers as she could.

Suddenly, there was a loud explosion, and the whole diner shook. John looked up, his heart racing, and saw that one of the extremists had thrown a grenade into the building.

"Get down!" he shouted, diving behind a table.

The explosion rocked the diner, sending debris flying everywhere. John could feel the heat of the blast on his skin, and he knew that they were in serious trouble.

But even as the dust settled, they refused to give up. Tom picked himself up off the ground, his gun still in his hand, and looked around at Emma and John.

"We can't let them win," Tom said. "We have to keep fighting." Emma, Daniel and John nodded in agreement, and they resumed their positions, ready to continue the fight.

The battle raged on for what felt like hours. In the end, Emma's side emerged victorious, but not without cost. Dr. Marberg and Tom were wounded, but not series. Simultaneously, Daniel's mind raced with thoughts of what they would do next and how they could possibly stop the extremists before it was too late. He knew that the investigation had become more and more dangerous than he ever could have imagined, and he knew that they were in for a long, hard fight.

11

The Bright Dawn Movement

Emma and her team gathered in their hotel room, tired and shaken from the events of the past few days. The room was littered with maps, tablets, laptops, and files, evidence of their investigation into the bioterrorism attack.

"We need to figure out who is behind this," Emma said, her voice hoarse from all the shouting and fighting. "We have to stop them."

"Yeah, but where do we even start?" Mike asked, rubbing his tired eyes.

"We start with what we know," Emma replied. "The virus was developed in the PathogenX Lab we raided. And we know that the extremists are involved somehow. We need to find out how they're connected and why they're doing this."

"But how do we find that out?" Sarah asked.

"We go back to the facility," John suggested. "We need to search it more thoroughly, see if we can find anything that will give us a lead."

John's proposal stunned everyone in the room.

"And what about the extremists?" Mike asked after a long while. "They're not going to just sit back and let us do our thing."

John sighed. "I know. We'll have to be careful. But we can't let them stop us."

The team worked late into the night, pouring over documents, analyzing data, and planning their next move. As the sun began to rise, they finally came up with a plan. They would split up into two groups. Emma, Mike, Sarah and John would return to the PathogenX Lab, while the others would try to track down any leads on the extremists.

As they made their way to the facility, Emma's nerves were on edge. She couldn't shake the feeling that they were walking into a trap. Once they arrived, they split up, searching every nook and cranny for any clues. It wasn't long before Sarah let out a cry of triumph.

"I found something! I found something!" she exclaimed.

The rest of the team rushed over to where she was standing. She was holding a file labeled "Extremist Connection."

They quickly scanned through the file, trying to absorb as much information as possible. They formed an organization called "The Bright Dawn Movement". Its aim was focused on bringing about a new era and a new beginning to the world through Virocide X they created. It also detailed how they had been working with the researchers to develop Virocide X, using it as a means to further their extremist agenda.

As they read on, they realized that the situation was even worse than they had imagined. The virus was highly contagious and deadly, and it had already been planned to spread to multiple countries in a couple of weeks.

"We have to stop them," Sarah said, her voice trembling with anger. "We can't let them get away with this."

They quickly gathered all the evidence they could find and made their way back to their hotel room. They spent the rest of the day analyzing the data, trying to come up with a plan to stop the bioterrorists.

As the night wore on, they grew more and more frustrated. They believed that they might be up against a well-funded and well-organized group.

"We need a miracle," Daniel muttered, staring at his laptop screen.

But Emma wasn't ready to give up yet. "We'll find a way," she said, her voice full of determination. "We need to, we have to."

With that, the team got back to work, determined to prevent a global catastrophe. As the team continued their discussion, they couldn't help but feel a growing sense of urgency. They needed to act quickly if they were going to prevent a global catastrophe. Emma looked around the room at her team, each of them focused on the task at hand, and felt a wave of gratitude. They were the best of the best, and she knew they would stop at nothing to get to the bottom of this.

"Hey guys, I have a suggestion," Emma spoke up.

"I'm listening," Daniel replied.

"We need to get in touch with the US government," Emma said, breaking the silence. "We can't do this alone. We need their resources and expertise."

"Right, I'll make the call," Tom answered, reaching for his smart phone. "Um……, but we need to be careful. We don't know who we can trust."

Emma nodded in agreement. "We need to keep our guard up at all times. The extremists have proven that they will stop at nothing to protect their interests."

The team spent the next several hours brainstorming and strategizing. They discussed possible leads and avenues of investigation, debated the best course of action, and tried to anticipate the moves of their enemies. As the sun began to set outside, they looked up at the clock and realized they had been at it for over ten hours.

"We need to take a break," Maria said, stretching her cramped muscles. "We'll reconvene in a few hours, after we've had a chance to rest and recharge."

The team agreed, and one by one, they gathered their things and headed out of the room. Emma lingered behind, taking one last look around the table. This was it, she thought to herself. The moment of truth. It seemed that the fate of the world rested in their hands. With a deep breath, she turned and followed her team out of the room, ready to face whatever lay ahead.

12

The First Step

The team arrived in Washington DC late in the evening, exhausted from the long trip. They checked into a hotel and got some much-needed rest. The next day, they dressed in their best suits and headed to the Department of Homeland Security to meet with the officials.

As they entered the building, they felt nervous. They were about to brief some of the most powerful people in the country on a potential bioterrorism attack, and she knew they would face resistance and skepticism.

The team was escorted into a spacious conference room, with a large wooden table dominating the center of the space. The walls were painted in a calming shade of blue, and large windows let in a flood of natural light, illuminating the room. Several officials were already seated around the table, their faces stern and serious.

Emma couldn't help but feel a sense of apprehension as she recognized a few of them from news reports. She tried to steady her nerves, reminding herself that they were here for a reason, and that they needed to remain focused and alert.

The chairs around the table were comfortable and upholstered in dark leather, and the room was equipped with the latest technology – large screens displayed data and charts, while microphones and speakers dotted the table.

As they took their seats, they couldn't help but feel a sense of awe at the gravity of their situation. They were now in the heart of the government's response efforts, and the fate of millions rested on their shoulders.

"Good morning, Dr. Lee," one of the officials greeted her. "I'm Director Mr. Carl Johnson, and this is our team. We've been briefed on your situation, but we'd like to hear more about it from you."

Emma took a deep breath and began her presentation. She explained their investigation, the evidence they had gathered, and their theory that a bioterrorism attack was underway. She could feel the tension in the room as she spoke, and she could see the skepticism in the eyes of some of the officials.

"Dr. Lee, with all due respect, this sounds like quite a leap in logic," one of the officials spoke up. "Are you sure there's not a more rational explanation for the cases you've seen?"

Emma felt a wave of frustration wash over her. How could they not see the evidence right in front of them?

"With all due respect, Director Johnson, we've seen enough evidence to suggest that this is not a natural occurrence," Emma replied firmly. "We believe that a bioterrorism attack is underway, and we need your help to stop it."

The officials looked at each other, clearly unsure of what to do. Finally, Director Johnson spoke up.

"Dr. Lee, we appreciate your concern, but you have to understand that these are serious accusations. We can't just launch an investigation based on a theory. We need hard evidence."

The team knew that this was the moment they had been preparing for. Emma pulled out a folder from her briefcase and placed it on the table in front of her.

"Director Johnson, I understand your concerns. That's why we've compiled a dossier of all the evidence we've gathered so far," Emma explained, opening the folder. "We have medical records, eyewitness accounts, and even samples of the virus. The virus's name is Virocide X. We've also tracked down the source of the virus, and we know who's responsible. In short, we sneaked in the PathogenX Lab of the Innovatech Research Institute, and we found documents showing that Virocide X was created by some advanced genetic engineering techniques there, just a month or a few weeks ago. This is a man-made virus. Actually, we've found more. We know that a crazy group of extremists called "The Bright Dawn Movement" gives birth to this Virocide X and its primary goal is to clean the world by this deadly virus."

"**THIS IS A BIOWEAPON**," Emma said, her voice barely above a whisper.

The officials leaned forward in their seats, their interest piqued. Emma continued to present their findings, detailing the steps they had taken to track down the terrorists responsible for the attack. She could see the skepticism melting away as she spoke, replaced by a growing sense of concern. Finally, Emma concluded her presentation, and the room fell silent. The officials looked at each other, clearly unsure of what to do next.

Director Johnson and the officials needed further discussion, and after several hours of detailed deliberation and consideration, they arrived at a conclusion.

"Dr. Lee, this is quite a revelation," Director Johnson said finally. "We need to take this very seriously. I'm going to have my team start an investigation immediately, and I'll be sure to keep you updated on our progress."

Emma breathed a sigh of relief. They had done it. They had convinced the officials to take action. As they left the conference room, the team breathed a collective sigh of relief. They knew they had a long way to go to stop the bioterrorism attack, but they had taken the first step.

As the investigation into the Virocide X virus started, it became clear that the PathogenX Laboratory had been involved in its production. The Department of Homeland Security moved quickly, closing down the lab and arresting all scientists involved in the development of the deadly virus in the next day.

Emma and her team were stunned by the news.

"We did it," Mike said, grinning at his team.

"I can't believe we actually did it," said Sarah, grinning from ear to ear.

"It wasn't easy," replied Emma, "but we did what we had to do."

"I think we should celebrate," said Daniel. "What do you say we grab some dinner and drinks?"

Emma nodded in agreement. "That sounds like a good idea. We could all use a little break."

They found a nearby restaurant and settled in for a well-deserved meal. As they ate and drank, they felt a sense of camaraderie and accomplishment. They had faced incredible challenges and overcome seemingly insurmountable obstacles, and they had done it together.

But even as they celebrated, they knew that their work was far from over. The clock was ticking, and every passing moment brought them closer and closer to a global catastrophe. They would need to stay focused and work tirelessly if they had any hope of stopping the terrorists and saving countless lives.

As they left the restaurant and headed back to their hotel, Emma had a sense of anxiety creeping up on her. She knew that the next steps would be crucial, and the stakes had never been higher. She would need to rely on her team, her training, and her instincts if they were going to succeed.

13

Decrypting Danger

Although the PathogenX Laboratory was shut down, the dissemination of Virocide X did not cease. The government suspected that the Bright Dawn Movement had established an alternative facility for the manufacture of the virus.

Sitting in her hotel room, Emma stared fixedly at the computer screen before her. Her team had been assigned with the daunting challenge of identifying and bringing to justice the Bright Dawn Movement who were accountable for releasing Virocide X virus at multiple locations throughout the country, along with discovering a cure for it. Despite the enormity of the mission, she was resolute in her determination to see it through to its conclusion.

That's when she received a message from a group of military and intelligence operatives who claimed to have information on the whereabouts of the Bright Dawn Movement. Emma was skeptical at first, but after a few phone calls and a meeting with the team, she knew that they were the real deal.

The team shared what little information they had – a series of obscure clues that had led them to believe that the extremists were hiding out on a remote island in the Pacific. Emma, Maria, Tom and John immediately went to work, piecing together the clues and trying to find any potential leads.

"We know that they've been using a lot of encrypted communication," Emma said to Tom and John as they pored over satellite images of the island. "We need to find a way to break through their encryption and see what they're saying."

"I might be able to help with that," said Albert Chadwick, one of the intelligence operatives. "I have a contact who's an expert in encryption breaking. I can reach out to him and see if he can get us any further information."

Emma turned to the Albert, intrigued. "Who's your contact?" she asked.

Albert hesitated for a moment before responding. "His name is David Newton," he said. "He's one of the best in the business when it comes to encryption breaking."

Tom impressed. "Alright, let's get in touch with him and see what he can do."

Albert pulled out his smart phone immediately and began typing a few messages. After a few moments, he looked up at Emma. "He'll be in touch soon," he said.

Sure enough, just a few hours later, Emma received an email from David. He had managed to crack into some of the extremists' communications and had found evidence suggesting that they were indeed on the remote island in the Pacific.

"This is great news," Emma said with excitement. "But we need more information. Can you keep working on this and see if you can find out where exactly on the island they might be?"

David responded quickly through another email. "I'll do my best," he said. "But it won't be easy. They're using some pretty advanced encryption methods."

Emma smiled. "I have faith in you," she said. "Just keep me updated on any further developments."

Over the next few days, David worked tirelessly to break through the extremists' encryption. He kept the team informed every step of the way, sending Emma's regular updates on what he had managed to uncover.

Finally, after several long nights of work, David sent Emma a message with coordinates that he believed to be the location of the extremists' base – Babeldaob, an island in the Pacific.

"We need to act on this now," Emma said to her buddies as they prepared to launch their raid. "This is our chance to take down these terrorists once and for all."

"They're using a network of caves as their base of operations," Emma said, making on their way towards Babeldaob and reading the decrypted messages. "We need to figure out which cave they're in and launch a raid." They planned their operation. This was a high-risk mission, and there were no guarantees that they would succeed. But they knew that it was their duty to try.

The high-tech equipment was essential for this mission. They had advanced artibees, called "BeeWatch", a new technology of artificial mechanical bee, equipped with thermal imaging and infrared cameras to scout the area and detect any threats or movements. They also had portable scanners capable of analyzing and identifying Virocide X within minutes. These scanners were equipped with the latest technology, including polymerase chain reaction (PCR) machines, gene sequencing devices, and advanced microscopes. Additionally, they had specialized gear to protect themselves from Virocide X, including suits, respirators, and gloves.

As dawn broke, they loaded their equipment onto their transport planes and set off on their mission. The artibees were sent ahead to scout the area and map out the layout of the caves. The team used the information from BeeWatches to create a detailed map of search, taking into account any potential threats, obstacles, or hazards.

14

The Island Storm and Hostile Welcome

The team approached Babeldaob with caution, knowing that they could face unexpected obstacles. They had prepared for the worst, but they could never have anticipated the storm that was brewing.

The storm that descended upon the team was unlike any they had ever encountered. The wind howled around them, shaking the boat violently from side to side. Waves crashed against the sides of the vessel, sending it pitching and rolling through the water. Rain poured down in sheets, driving into their faces and making it impossible to see more than a few feet ahead. The lightning flashed bright and sudden, illuminating the dark sky for brief moments before fading back into the blackness.

As Daniel and Tom fought to keep the boat under control, they realized with growing concern that they were quickly losing ground. The storm was too powerful, too relentless, and they were at its mercy. Every time they thought they had gained some measure of stability, a massive wave would come crashing over the bow, throwing them off balance once again. They knew that if they didn't find shelter soon, they risked being tossed overboard and lost to the fury of the storm.

Luckily, they spotted a small cove ahead and managed to steer the boat into it. The cove provided some shelter from the storm, but they were still not safe. The winds howled around them, and the waves crashed against the rocks, threatening to capsize the boat.

They huddled together, trying to stay warm and dry.

As the storm raged on, they realized that they had to adapt to their environment. They brought out their equipment, designed to withstand extreme weather conditions. They used a BeeWatch to survey the area, looking for any signs of life or activity on the island.

The artibee provided a bird's-eye view of the island, revealing that there were some structures built into the hillside, likely to protect them from the wind and rain. They made the decision to brave the storm and make their way to the structures, hoping to find shelter.

As they made their way up the hillside, they encountered some unexpected obstacles. Some locals had noticed their arrival and were not pleased. They blocked the team's path, armed with machetes and other makeshift weapons. It was clear that they were not going to let the outsiders pass. Sarah tried to reason with them, explaining that they were there to stop a global catastrophe and that they needed their help.

But she failed, the locals were not convinced. They had been living on the island for generations and were fiercely protective of their home. They believed that the outsiders were there to take something from them, and they were not going to let that happen.

Daniel looked around at Emma, Maria, and Laura. "We've got a problem," he said. "The locals are not going to easily trust us."

Maria agreed. "They're protective of their island," she said. "We need to find a way to show them that we're not here to harm them."

Emma thought for a moment before speaking up. "What if we use our high-tech equipment to impress and persuade them?" she suggested.

Laura raised an eyebrow. "How do you mean?" she asked.

"Well, we could set up a demonstration," Emma explained. "Show them what our equipment can do, how it can help them protect their island from Virocide X."

Daniel nodded. "That's a good idea," he said. "But we need to make sure that we're respectful of their culture and customs while we do it."

Maria agreed. "We'll need to approach this carefully," she said. "We don't want to come across as threatening or imposing."

As they approached the group of hostile locals, Emma raised her hands in a gesture of peace. "We are not here to harm you or your island," she said calmly. "We are here to help."

One of the locals stepped forward, his hand on his machete. "Why should we believe you?" he asked with a loud voice.

Emma motioned to the team to bring out the high-tech equipment. They unveiled their artibees, scanners, and other devices, explaining how each of them could help protect the island. The locals watched in amazement as the devices were activated and demonstrated.

"We have the technology to detect and neutralize the virus that threatens your island," Emma said. "We need your help to do it."

The locals looked at each other, still unsure. Emma could see that they were considering her proposal, but they needed more convincing.

"We know that you have been protecting your island for generations," Emma continued. "We respect that, and we want to help you continue to do so. But we need your cooperation to succeed."

One of the elders of the group stepped forward, his eyes locked onto Emma's. "What do you need from us?" he asked.

"We need your knowledge of the island," Emma replied. "We need to work together to find a group of men hiding in some caves now before they're going to hurt you."

The elder looked at Emma for a moment longer before nodding his head. "We will help you," he said. "But you must promise that you will not betray our trust."

Emma assented. "We promise," she said. "We will work together to protect your island."

With the locals now on their side, the team continued their journey through the storm towards the shores of Babeldaob. Days later, they made their way inland, sticking to the shadows and keeping a close eye out for any signs of danger. With the analysis from the BeeWatches, it wasn't long before they found the entrance to a cave system. They crept inside, guns at the ready, and began to search for any signs of extremists from the Bright Dawn Movement.

15

The Lucky Break

As they approached the entrance of the cave system, they noticed that it was heavily guarded. They decided to use their high-tech equipment to scan the area for any hidden traps or explosives. After a thorough scan, they determined that there were no traps in the immediate vicinity, so they cautiously made their way towards the entrance.

As they got closer, they noticed that two guards were heavily armed and appeared to be on high alert. They quickly realized that this was going to be a challenge. John knew that they needed to find a way to knock down the guards without alerting them.

"Let Sarah and I pretend to be a lost couple, arguing over who was responsible for taking the wrong path as we walk. Then, I look for an opportunity to take them down," John explained his plan.

"Let's do it!" Sarah agreed.

Sarah and John approached the gate, trying to look as natural as possible. As they neared the guards, Sarah's heart began to race. She wasn't sure if their distraction would work, but they had no other choice. They had to get past the guards if they wanted to succeed.

As they got closer, Sarah and John began to argue loudly, attracting the guards' attention. "I told you we should have gone left!" Sarah yelled, hoping to create a believable argument. "No, you said we should have gone right!" John retorted, playing along.

The guards turned to look at them, their expressions wary. "What's going on here?" one of them demanded.

Sarah stepped forward, trying to look as annoyed as possible. "We're lost," she said, gesturing to John. "He won't listen to me and we've been walking in circles for hours."

The guards exchanged a look, but didn't lower their weapons. "You're not supposed to be here," one of them said, eyeing Sarah and John suspiciously.

Sarah tried to think quickly. "We know that," she said, feigning exasperation. "That's why we're trying to find our way out. Look, we don't want any trouble. Just tell us the way we should go and we'll leave."

The two guards hesitated, looking uncertain. Sarah could feel her heart pounding in her chest. This was it. If they didn't convince the guards to let them go, their entire mission would be jeopardized.

The two guards still hesitated…

Before the hesitation ended, John dashed forward like a gust of wind. He extended his right arm and struck one of the guard's right temple, causing him to faint immediately. Then, John swiftly grabbed the other guard's wrists and twisted them, causing the gun to fall to the ground. In the blink of an eye, he followed up with an elbow strike to that guard's head, causing him to kneel before fainting as well. John knocked them down in just two seconds!

Ten seconds passed.

"Wonderful attack. You are really a superman!" Sarah breathed a sigh of relief. John ignored her appreciation and frisked the two guards' bodies.

"Done!" John said when he got a key. John approached the door and unlocked it quickly.

"Go, go, go!" John called Sarah. She returned to her senses at this moment and the team slipped inside successfully.

Once inside the facility, no security personnel were visible, but the team encountered various traps and obstacles. They came across several rooms that were booby-trapped with explosive devices. They carefully navigated their way through the maze of traps, using their high-tech equipment to detect any hidden explosives.

As Emma and her team progressed deeper into the facility, they came across another obstacle. The corridor ahead was enveloped in a dense fog that posed a new challenge to their mission. The extent of the fog made it nearly impossible for them to see more than a couple of feet in front of them, raising the possibility of potential danger ahead.

The team was aware that this could be a trap set up by the Bright Dawn Movement to impede their progress. They quickly strategized and decided to bring out their gas masks and night-vision goggles to navigate their way through the murky haze. Donning their protective gear, they were now able to see more clearly and had a better view of what lay ahead of them.

Moving cautiously forward, they kept their weapons ready and senses heightened, expecting the unexpected. The thick mists seemed to cling to everything, making it difficult to get a clear reading on their surroundings. They continued to make slow but steady progress, with each step taking them closer to their goal.

Finally, after fifteen minutes of navigating through traps and obstacles, they reached the heart of the facility. They discovered a laboratory filled with test tubes and other equipment, and they knew that they were getting closer to the extremists.

They continued to explore the laboratory and noticed that there was a super quantum computer system that was still active. Emma quickly hacked into the system and downloaded all of the information that she could find. However, the hack triggered the explosive system of the room and its exit closed. The laboratory blew up in five minutes.

They frantically searched the room, scanning every inch for any sign of a switch or a button that could open the door.

"Guys, we've got to hurry," Mike shouted. "We don't have much time left! Two minutes left!"

As they searched, they noticed a small panel on the wall. John approached it and began typing furiously on his laptop.

"I think I've found the code to open the door," John said. "But it's going to take me a few minutes to hack into the system."

"We don't have enough time!" Tom exclaimed. "Is there any way to speed it up?"

John shook his head. "I'm working as fast as I can, but this is a complicated system."

Suddenly, they heard a loud beep, followed by a robotic voice.

"Final warning. Final warning. Explosives activated. Two minutes until detonation." The team started to panic. They knew that they had to act fast if they wanted to make it out alive.

"Come on, John!" Emma and Laura yelled. "We need to get out of here now!"

John's fingers flew over the keyboard as he desperately tried to hack into the system. Finally, he managed to crack the code.

"I did it! I did it!" John yelled. "The door is open now."

Emma breathed a sigh of relief as they rushed out of the room. They had ninety seconds left, so they ran down the hallway, following the signs towards the facility's exit.

"We're almost there," Emma said. "Just a little further." They burst through the door and ran towards their van. As they left the facility a few seconds, they could see it exploding in the distance.

"This is a trap. They're aware of our presence here. We are lucky," Daniel sighed.

"Yes, we are just lucky," Maria echoed.

As Emma's team rushed towards their van, they heard gunshots coming from somewhere nearby. They knew that they had to be careful as there was a possibility that the attackers might come after them.

Just as they were getting closer to the vehicle, they were suddenly confronted by a middle-aged man with salt-and-pepper hair and a young lady with long curly hair and intense brown eyes. The two were accompanied by several armed men who aimed their guns at the team.

"Hahaha! What do we have here? It seems like we have some unwanted guests," the young lady sneered.

"Who are you people? What are you doing here?" the man demanded to know.

"We're just passing through. We heard the explosion and we're trying to get out of here as soon as possible," Daniel explained, hoping to buy some time.

"You're lying. I can tell by the way you're talking. You're here to investigate us, aren't you?" the lady accused.

Realizing that they couldn't lie anymore, Daniel decided to ask a question.

"May I ask you a question?" he requested.

"Who are you? It seems to me that you know something about us," Daniel asked.

The man and the lady exchanged a glance before the man sneered and replied, "Fine! Before you die, I might as well tell you. Yes, we know who you are. You're WHO investigators who have been investigating the events surrounding the Virocide X virus, including who created it and where their base is located. You hope to catch them all and find its cure, right?"

The team had no response, but inside they couldn't help but wonder how these strangers seemed to know everything about their investigation.

Sarah stepped forward, her anger and disbelief etched on her face, and shouted, "You can't just decide who deserves to live and who doesn't."

"Oh, but we can. And we will. The world needs to be cleansed, and Virocide X is just the beginning," the man laughed loudly.

Emma clenched her fists, her eyes locked on the man and the lady. "You're insane. You have no right to play God with people's lives."

"Hahaha, right and wrong are just concepts, my dear. In the grand scheme of things, they mean nothing. All that matters is power. And with this virus, we have the power to shape the world as we see fit," the lady laughed too.

The team members bristled with anger, but they knew that they couldn't do anything to stop them. The armed men loaded their guns and pointed them at the team, causing every member's face to show a look of despair, thinking that everything was about to come to an end.

Emma and her team tensed up, ready for the last battle, a battle that was certain to be lost. But before they could react, there was a deafening explosion behind their enemies. The team members immediately crouched down, covering their heads. They only glanced up for a moment and saw a group of soldiers in uniform, led by a big man, fighting the enemies with intense gunfire.

After several minutes of melee, when the dust settled, everything returned to calm, they could see that the man and woman had been subdued and were pinned to the ground. Their gunmen had been killed by the group of soldiers. The team members looked around in confusion, unsure of what had just happened.

Then they heard a voice behind them.

"Are you all okay? We received Dr. Lee's distress signal and came as quickly as we could," he explained. "My name is Captain Gilbert. We're here to take you to safety."

Emma's team nodded gratefully, still in shock from the sudden turn of events.

"Is everyone okay? Anyone hurt?" Emma asked, making sure that everyone was accounted for.

"I'm fine. Just a scratch," Tom answered.

"Me too. Thank goodness we made it out alive," Laura said.

With the battle won, Emma turned to the man and woman who were lying on the ground, defeated. "It's over," she said. "You've lost."

The man let out a bitter laugh. "You think this is the end? You have no idea what's coming. Virocide X was just the beginning. You can't stop us. **Virus saves the world! Virus saves the world!**"

Emma's team members exchanged glances, knowing that they had won this battle but realizing that there could be more challenges ahead. They knew that they had to stay vigilant and always be ready to face whatever threat may come their way.

"Take them back to our place. We need to ask them questions," Emma said to Mike and John.

16

The Interrogation

Mike and Maria apprehended the man and woman and took them into custody. The two were then brought to a secure location where they would be interrogated. Emma's team was able to identify the suspects by searching their bodies. The man was identified as Mr. Oliver Jensen who is a wealthy businessman. The young lady was Dr. Maya Gupta, a brilliant scientist and microbiology expert. They were suspected to be some important members of the Bright Dawn Movement.

John was assigned to interrogate Oliver. He stood across from him, his eyes locked onto him, determined to get answers no matter what it took.

"Mr. Oliver, I know that you are one of the leaders of your extremists. Why did you do this?" John demanded. "You are a rich man. Why did you create Virocide X virus and unleash it on innocent people?"

Oliver smirked. "You are John, right? You'll never understand. You're too blinded by your moral compass to see the truth."

John clenched his fists. "Try me."

Oliver leaned back in his chair. "The world is corrupt and diseased. It's filled with people who are unworthy of life. They're polluting the planet, destroying the environment, and causing chaos. We wanted to create a new world order, a world where only the strongest and most deserving survive. **Virus saves the world!**"

John shook his head in disbelief. "You can't just decide who deserves to live and who doesn't. That's not your decision to make."

Oliver sneered. "It is now. And you, John, you and your team are nothing but pests. You're standing in the way of progress. But don't worry, we have a plan for you too."

John's heart sank. "What plan?"

Oliver's smile grew wider. "Let's just say that you won't be a problem for much longer."

John's blood ran cold. He knew that Oliver was not bluffing. He needed to act fast.

"Tell me, Oliver," John said. "Where is the antidote? We know that you have it."

Oliver's expression grew darker. "Why should I tell you?"

"Because if you don't, then you'll die here and now," John replied, his voice cold and determined.

"I've prepared for this. Abra cadabra! Abra cadabra!" Oliver shouted.

John was unable to comprehend Oliver's words. Suddenly, Oliver began convulsing and shouting "Abra cadabra" twice. His eyes rolled back, and he foamed at the mouth, leaving John bewildered. Realizing the gravity of the situation, John promptly alerted other members of his team for assistance. Sadly, it was too late as Oliver passed away within a minute.

After a thorough examination by the doctors, Oliver's cause of death was determined to be poisoning related to the phrase 'Abra cadabra' he shouted before his death. Emma then interrogated Maya for confirmation.

"I'm Emma, the team leader. I've bad news for you. Your companion just died a few minutes ago. I'm sorry for your loss. His last word is 'Abra cadabra'. I want to ask you some questions," Emma said.

"It is an incantation, an incantation …" Maya kept repeating in a whispery voice.

"What is it? Can you explain?" Emma asked.

Maya hesitated for a long moment before relenting. "I need to be free. I don't want to die. This is my request," Maya replied to Emma with a trembling tone.

Emma nodded. "You have my word. Go ahead."

"Abra cadabra is an incantation.[1] Each member in the group has been implanted with a nanobot. If we or our boss say the phrase twice, the bot will release a poison inside us that can kill an elephant. We will die within one minute," Maya explained.

"Remove the bot from my body," Maya requested.

"The top scientists and engineers will save you, without a doubt. However, I need more information about the group," Emma assured.

Maya continued. "The Bright Dawn Movement consists of five core members. We are two of them. Oliver is a good man. He is a wealthy businessman who supported our group financially and provided us with resources. He

---

[1] It is Latin. Historically, it has been associated with various cultural and religious practices. Its first known occurrence is in the second-century works of Serenus Sammonicus.

sees himself as a visionary and a futurist, and believes that the virus is a necessary step in human evolution. Oliver uses his influence and wealth to further the group's goals."

"Who are the other members? Who is the boss?" Emma asked.

"Carlos, he is a soldier, and Rachel, an idealistic activist. Our boss called himself Gabriel. He is mid-40, I guess. He is responsible for creating and releasing the virus. He has a magnetic personality that draws people to him, and he uses his charm to persuade us to follow his extremist ideology. Gabriel sees himself as a savior of the planet and believes that wiping out most of humanity is the only way to save the Earth from destruction," Maya said.

"I joined Gabriel's group after becoming disillusioned with the scientific community's lack of action on climate change. I just want to save the environment. I think he can help me through the virus," Maya continued, tears streaming down her face.

Emma was convinced that Maya had nothing to hide, so she ordered her to be taken back to jail in Washington DC, waiting for an operation of bot removal later. The team hoped to extract valuable information from the bot.

Emma's heart was racing with anxiety. She knew that Gabriel posed a substantial threat to everyone and everything with his twisted worldview. As she left the interrogation room, she realized that they had to act fast. They had to locate Gabriel and put an end to his plan, but she didn't know how…

17

Chaos in Cities over the World

The team quickly made their way to the helicopters and took off, leaving Babeldaob behind. As they gained altitude, Emma felt a sense of relief that they had accomplished part of the mission. However, her relief was short-lived as they received a distress signal from their headquarters.

"What's going on?" Emma asked as she listened to the transmission.

"It's chaos," came the voice of Mr. Carl Johnson, the Director of the Department of Homeland Security. "Virocide X has spread worldwide, and people are panicking. We need you back here now."

Emma's heart sank as she realized the gravity of the situation. "Understood," she replied. "We're on our way."

Two days later, as they flew towards Washington DC, they could see the chaos unfolding below them. Cities were in disarray, people were running in all directions, and emergency services were overwhelmed. The team knew that this was the work of Gabriel, who had managed to spread the virus globally.

Once they landed on the rooftop of the headquarter, the team rushed to their director's office, where they found him surrounded by maps and reports.

"We're facing a global pandemic," Johnson said as they entered. "Virocide X has spread to every corner of the world, and we're already seeing the effects of the virus on a global scale, and it's only going to get worse. We're struggling to keep up with the demand for supplies and medical personnel."

"For examples, take a look at the reports of the cities of Tokyo, Toronto, and Rome," Johnson continued.

In Tokyo, crowds of people panicked as they heard reports of the virus's deadly effects. The streets were filled with people wearing masks and gloves, trying to protect themselves from the virus. Shops quickly sold out of supplies such as hand sanitizer, masks, and disinfectant, leaving many people desperate and afraid. Public transportation systems ground to a halt as people refused to ride trains or buses for fear of infection. Hospitals became overcrowded as those who felt ill flocked to seek medical attention, causing long waiting times and straining the resources of healthcare workers.

Meanwhile, in Toronto, fear and uncertainty gripped the city completely. People rushed to stock up on food and other supplies, leading to empty shelves in supermarkets and stores. Panic spread rapidly as rumors and misinformation circulated about the virus, causing many people to distrust official sources of information. Many businesses closed their doors, causing widespread economic disruption and job losses. Despite government efforts to calm the public and provide support, the situation only seemed to get worse as the days went on.

In Rome, the situation was similar. The streets were eerily quiet as people stayed indoors to avoid infection. Schools, colleges and universities shut down, and many workplaces closed as employees were told to work from home. People hoarded supplies, and there were reports of fights breaking out over basic essentials such as toilet paper. The city's hospitals struggled to cope with the influx of patients, and healthcare workers faced increased risk of infection due to shortages of protective equipment.

As Virocide X continued to spread, the situation in these cities grew increasingly dire. The fear and uncertainty caused by the pandemic had a profound impact on people's mental health, with many reporting feelings of anxiety and dread. In addition to the physical toll of the virus, there was a growing sense of social isolation and disconnection.

Daniel and Tom felt a sense of anger and frustration as they listened to Johnson's words. This was exactly what Gabriel had wanted – chaos and destruction on a global scale.

"What can we do to stop this?" Emma asked.

Johnson looked at the team with a grave expression. "We need to find a cure," he said. "And fast. We've assembled the best minds in medicine and science, but we're still struggling to come up with a solution."

Emma met his gaze steadily. "We'll do whatever it takes to help. We won't let you down," she said.

18
The Search for a Virocide X Antidote

The team was working on a cure for Virocide X in a medical laboratory in Washington DC. The serum that they were working on was a complex mixture of various compounds, each carefully selected for its potential to counteract Virocide X. The team had spent several weeks researching and testing different compounds, and they had narrowed down their choices to a handful of promising candidates.

The first compound they had used was a potent antiviral agent that had shown promise in previous trials. This compound was designed to attack Virocide X directly, preventing it from replicating and spreading throughout the body. Although it had shown some success in the initial rounds of testing, it had failed to produce the desired results in the latest batch of experiments.

"Laura, have you seen the results of the latest batch of experiments with the antiviral compound?" Daniel asked.

"Yes, I have. Unfortunately, it didn't produce the desired results," Laura replied.

"That's disappointing. This compound showed promise in previous trials. What could be the reason for its failure this time?" Daniel sighed.

"It's hard to say at this point. We may need to re-evaluate the dosage and administration of the compound," Maria answered.

"Do you think we should abandon this compound altogether and focus on a new approach?" Daniel suggested.

"I think we should give up on it and try another approach," Emma said.

The second compound they had tried was a powerful immunomodulator that was designed to boost the body's immune response to Virocide X. This compound was intended to help the body fight off Virocide X more effectively, reducing the severity and duration of the infection.

"Guys, the results from the latest batch of experiments with the immunomodulator compound are in. Unfortunately, we still didn't see any significant improvements," Laura said.

"That's really frustrating. We were hoping this compound would be the breakthrough we need to fight Virocide X," Mike moaned.

"Do you think we should abandon this approach altogether?" Maria asked.

"We can't give up just yet. We need to keep exploring all our options," Laura replied.

"Agreed. But we also need to figure out why this compound isn't working. Are there any possible reasons that we haven't considered?" Daniel said.

"Well, one possibility is that the dosage isn't right. Maybe we need to adjust it and try again," Laura proposed.

"What about the administration? Could we try a different delivery method?" Mike wondered.

"Or maybe there's something about Virocide X that we don't fully understand. Perhaps we need to investigate further," Maria advised.

"These are all good points. Let's explore each option and see if we can come up with a plan for the next round of testing," Daniel said.

However, this compound had also failed to produce any noticeable results in the latest batch of modified experiments they did.

The third and final compound they had used was a new experimental drug that had shown promise in treating other viral infections. This drug worked by targeting a specific enzyme that was essential for the virus to replicate. By inhibiting this enzyme, the drug could effectively stop Virocide X from spreading throughout the body. Unfortunately, like the first and second compounds, it had failed to produce any significant results in the latest round of experiments.

Despite their disappointment, they refused to give up. They knew that developing a serum to counteract Virocide X was a challenging and complex task, and they were determined to see it through to the end. They would continue to research and test new compounds, hoping that the day they would find the breakthrough they needed to save the world from the virus's deadly grip came very soon.

Maria sighed heavily as she looked over the data from their latest experiment. "This isn't working," she said to her buddies. "We need to try something else."

"Maybe we're looking at this the wrong way," suggested Tom, an epidemiologist. "We've been trying to directly counteract Virocide X, but what if we tried to boost the immune system and prevent the virus from replicating at the same time instead? Give the body a fighting chance and time to fight off the virus on its own?"

Mike nodded thoughtfully, considering Tom's idea. "It's worth a shot," he said. "Let's get to work."

Over the next few days, they conducted a series of experiments to test Tom's theory. They tried different combinations of compounds and ran various tests to see how the immune system would respond.

At first, there were no notable results. Mike and Tom grew frustrated, knowing that time was running out to develop a viable solution. But they refused to give up, working long hours and experimenting with different approaches.

Finally, they found a combination of compounds that seemed to stimulate the immune system and deactivate the virus for a certain period of time effectively. The team was elated, knowing that they were finally making progress. But they knew that they still had a long way to go before they could produce a serum that would be effective on a global scale. They continued to conduct experiments, testing the serum on different strains of the virus and different animal subjects.

As they worked, the team began to grow closer, bonding over their shared determination to find a solution. They shared stories of their past experiences and joked with one another to keep their spirits high.

Despite the long hours and the setbacks they faced, the team was making progress. And they knew that they were working towards a cause greater than themselves – one that could potentially save countless lives around the world.

"We're getting closer," Emma said to the team one day. "I can feel it. We just need to keep pushing forward. Remember, no matter how long night, the arrival of daylight association."

"It's William Shakespeare," Maria said.

The team smiled and agreed firmly, ready to face whatever challenges lay ahead in their quest to find a cure.

19

The Lost Hope

Emma's team had a designated cleaning routine for their laboratory every night, but one Monday was different due to the absence of their regular cleaner. A replacement was provided, and they assumed it was standard procedure. However, this new cleaner behaved oddly by hiding several packages around the lab after completing the cleaning. That night, a massive explosion erupted, consuming everything in the laboratory. The firefighters worked tirelessly to extinguish the blaze, but the team's research results were lost totally. The police conducted an investigation and suspected the new cleaner's involvement, but this guy could not be caught.

Emma's team had been dealt another blow. The news of the destroyed laboratory hit them hard, and they were struggling to keep their spirits up. Emma knew that they needed to talk about it, so she called for a team meeting.

"Everyone, I know this news is hard to take," Emma began. "But we need to talk about how we're feeling and figure out what we can do next."

Tom spoke up. "I can't believe it. We've lost so much. How are we going to keep going?"

Emma took a deep breath before responding. "We'll keep going because we have to. We can't let these setbacks defeat us. We need to find another way, and we will."

Sarah spoke up. "But how? We've lost so much, and we're running out of options."

Emma looked around the room, taking in the defeat in her team's eyes. She knew that they needed a morale boost, something to give them hope.

"We'll figure it out," she said. "We've faced tough challenges before, and we've overcome them. We're a strong team, and we'll find a way to move forward. Don't give up and don't give in."

But despite Emma's words, the team was still struggling to come to terms with the loss of the laboratory. They had lost valuable resources, and they didn't know how they would continue without them.

Maria spoke up, tears streaming down her face. "We've been working so hard, and we keep getting knocked down. It's just not fair."

Emma could see the pain in her team's eyes, and her heart ached for them. She knew that they were exhausted, physically and emotionally. They needed a break, but there was no time for rest.

"We'll get through this," Emma said, her voice soft. "We'll keep going because we have to. We can't let the extremists win."

Laura spoke up, her voice wavering. "But what if we can't find a cure? What if we can't stop Virocide X?"

Emma knew that her team was feeling hopeless, but she refused to give up. She had to keep them motivated, keep them moving forward.

Emma's words echoed through the lab, stirring a renewed sense of determination in her team. They had been through so much, but Emma's unwavering resolve gave them the strength to carry on.

"We'll find a cure," Emma repeated, her voice growing stronger. "Guys, let's recall what we've encountered so far. We've been knocked down time and time again, but we always get back up. That's what sets us apart. We are scientists, and we are fighters. We are the master of the destiny. We can influence, direct and take control our own destiny. We can make it whatever you want it to be. Never give up until we find a solution."

The energy in the room was palpable as Emma continued to speak. Her words were like a rallying cry, galvanizing her team to push forward with renewed vigor.

"I know this setback hurts," Emma said, her voice softening slightly. "But we can't let it defeat us. We are stronger than this. We are stronger than anything that comes our way. We will find a way to overcome this, together."

They nodded in agreement, feeling their spirits lift as Emma spoke. They knew that they had a tough road ahead, but with Emma's leadership, they felt ready to face whatever challenges came their way.

"We'll get through this," Emma said, her voice filled with conviction. "And when we do, we'll have saved countless lives. We'll have made a difference in the world. So let's get back to work and make that difference. Let's show the world what we're made of. We're unique, nothing can replace us."

With those words, Emma turned and walked back to her lab bench, ready to dive back into her research. Her team followed suit, energized by Emma's speech and ready to take on whatever challenges lay ahead. They knew that they had a leader who would never give up, and that gave them the strength to keep going.

Emma's words seemed to give the team a glimmer of hope. They wiped away their tears and straightened their shoulders.

"You're right, Emma," John said. "We can do this. We'll find a way."

The team left the meeting, still feeling sad and defeated, but with a renewed sense of determination. Emma refused to let her team give up, they had come too far to let a setback stop them now.

20

Uncovering the Secrets of Virocide X

Emma's team was back at work in a new laboratory, but the loss of their previous laboratory still weighed heavily on them. They had lost not only their research results but also their equipment and supplies. Emma knew that they needed to speed up their search for a cure, but with limited resources, it seemed like an impossible task.

One day, as Emma was analyzing some data, she noticed something unusual. There appeared to be a pattern in the way the virus was mutating. She called a meeting with her team to discuss her findings.

"Guys, I think we might have found something," Emma said, her voice filled with excitement. "There seems to be a pattern in the way the virus is mutating. If we can understand this pattern, we might be able to develop a new approach to finding a cure."

Her team listened intently as Emma explained her discovery in detail. They were amazed at the potential implications of her findings.

"This could be huge," Tom said, his eyes lighting up. "If we can crack this code, we might be able to accelerate our search for a cure dramatically."

"But how do we go about cracking the code? We don't have the resources we need to do this kind of research," Sarah asked.

Laura thought for a moment before responding. "We might not have all the resources we need, but we do have something even more valuable – each other. We're a team, and we can pool our knowledge and expertise to tackle this problem together."

As the team delved deeper into their research, they became increasingly excited by their progress. They spent countless hours analyzing data and brainstorming ideas, and slowly but surely, they began to piece together the puzzle of Virocide X's mutations.

"This is incredible," Tom exclaimed one day as he examined some data. "I think we might be onto something big here."

Mike looked up from his own computer, a curious expression on his face. "What have you found?"

Tom quickly pulled up his screen and showed Mike the data. "Look at this – there's a spike here in the mutation rate. It's almost like it's trying to adapt to something."

Mike inclined thoughtfully. "Interesting. Let's run some more tests and see what we can find."

Over the next few days, the team worked tirelessly to test various theories and analyze data. As they continued to gather more information, they began to see patterns emerging. Slowly but surely, they were gaining a better understanding of how Virocide X worked and what made it so deadly.

"This is amazing," Maria said, her eyes wide with excitement. "We're really making progress."

Emma smiled, feeling a sense of pride wash over her. She had always known that her team was capable of great things, and now they were proving it beyond a shadow of a doubt.

But even as they worked tirelessly to unravel the mysteries of Virocide X, there were still setbacks and challenges along the way. One experiment failed spectacularly, leaving the team feeling defeated and frustrated.

"I don't understand," Sarah said, shaking her head in disbelief. "We've tried everything, and nothing seems to be working."

Emma put a hand on Sarah's shoulder, offering a reassuring smile. "It's okay. We'll figure this out. We've faced tough challenges before, and we've always managed to overcome them. This will be no different."

The team was energized by Emma's words, and they got straight back to work. They worked tirelessly over the next few weeks to unravel the mystery of Virocide X's behavior. They analyzed data, ran experiments, and collaborated on ideas. And finally, after many long hours of hard work, they had a breakthrough.

And slowly but surely, they began to see progress once again. Another breakthrough came one day when Laura noticed something unusual in the way the virus was spreading.

"Look at this," she said excitedly, pointing to a graph on her computer screen. "There's a pattern here. It's almost like Virocide X is targeting specific cells."

"I think we've found something," Emma said, her eyes shining with excitement. "If we target this specific protein, we might be able to neutralize the virus altogether." The team was amazed by Laura's discovery.

21

The Nanobot

Maya lay on an operating table in the Crystal Valley Regional Medical Center, her skin marked with lines indicating where the incision would be made. The room was cold and sterile, with bright lights shining down on the surgical team. Laura and Sarah stood off to the side, watching intently as the top scientists, doctors and engineers worked together to remove the nanobot from Maya's body.

After conducting a preliminary check and scan, the doctors determined that the nanobot was no bigger than a grain of rice. Despite its small size, it possessed the capability to wirelessly transmit sensitive information to its operators. This advanced piece of technology had been engineered to deliver lethal poison into the human body within a minute.

The high-tech structure of the nanobot was also truly remarkable. It consisted of a miniature computer chip, several tiny sensors, and a wireless transmitter. The chip was powered by a small battery.

The surgical team used state-of-the-art equipment to carefully cut into Maya's skin, making sure not to damage any vital organs or blood vessels. Once they reached the area where the nanobot was located, they used specialized tools to extract it from Maya's body. The nanobot was encased in a protective shell, which the team carefully removed to reveal the inner workings of the device.

Sarah looked over the shoulder of one of the scientists examining the nanobot. "What's so remarkable about it?" she asked.

The scientist turned to her, a look of awe on his face. "This is some of the most advanced technology I've ever seen," he said. "The level of miniaturization here is incredible. And the fact that it can transmit wirelessly without being detected is truly impressive."

Maya, who was lying on the operating table, groaned. "I don't care how impressive it is," she said. "Just get it out of me."

The surgeon chuckled. "Don't worry, Maya," he said. "We're almost done here. Just a few more minutes and we'll have this thing out of you."

As the team worked to carefully remove the nanobot from Maya's body, Laura continued to ask questions about its design.

"So, how long do you think this battery will last?" she asked.

The doctor looked up from his work. "Based on our analysis, it should be able to power the device for at least twenty years without needing to be replaced," he said.

Sarah raised an eyebrow. "Twenty years? That's incredible," she said. "Imagine what we could do with that kind of power source in other applications."

The doctor nodded. "Yes, it's certainly exciting to think about the possibilities," he said. "But for now, let's focus on getting this thing out of Maya safely."

As the surgical team examined the nanobot more closely, they realized that it was not a product of any domestic company. Their investigation led them to an international micro robot company that specialized in nanotechnology.

Emma's eyes widened as she heard the news. "An international micro robot company? Which one? Where is it?" she asked.

The lead scientist Dr. Georges Croll checked his notes. "It's called the Nano-Icosa International Corporation," he said. "They're based in Sweden and specialize in nanotechnology."

Emma made a mental note to look up more information about the company later. "Do we know who they created this nanobot for?" she asked.

Dr. Croll shook his head. "Not yet, but we're working on it," he said. "We're hoping to find some clues on the device itself or in the data that it transmitted."

Maya let out a sigh of relief. "I'm just grateful that it's out of me and I can move on with my life," she shouted.

As the team continued their investigation into the origins of the nanobot, Emma couldn't help but wonder the possible connection between Gabriel and the corporation. She was determined to do whatever it took to get to the truth, and she though they were closed to it.

22

Lab Attack Again

Emma sat at her desk in the lab, pouring over data on her computer screen. She had been up late the night before, trying to make sense of the results from the latest experiments. As she scrolled through the graphs and charts, her mind wandered to the possibility of the extremist group being behind the recent attacks on the labs. She couldn't shake the feeling that there was something important she was missing.

Suddenly, a loud explosion shook the building, causing Emma to jump up from her seat. She rushed to the door of the lab and peered out into the hallway. Chaos reigned outside as people ran past her, shouting and screaming. Emma's heart raced as she realized that her worst fears were coming true.

She quickly shut the door and turned to face her buddies, who were all gathered in the lab. "We need to move, now," she said, her voice steady despite her fear.

Daniel looked up from his microscope, confusion etched on his face. "What's going on?" he asked.

"There's been an attack on the lab again," Emma said, her eyes scanning the room. "We need to get out of here and regroup."

As she made her way through the scattered debris, she caught sight of three extremists, who were armed and clearly intent on causing as much destruction as possible.

“Stop right there!” Emma shouted, drawing her gun. “Put your weapons down and surrender.”

The leader dressed in black and sneered at her. “You think we’re just going to give up?” he said. “We’ve got a message for you: We’re not going to let anyone stand in our way. You know too much. Your team and lab must disappear in the world.”

“Your attempt will be futile! I promise!” Emma exclaimed boldly.

The two groups faced off, tension mounting as they stared each other down. Suddenly, one extremist opened fire, and chaos erupted as bullets flew through the air. Emma dove for cover, firing her weapon in return as she tried to protect her team and neutralize the threat. The sound of gunfire echoed throughout the building as the two sides engaged in a fierce battle.

The extremists had come prepared, with explosives and heavy weaponry that caused massive damage to the lab and endangered the lives of everyone inside. Emma knew that they needed to take action and fast if they were going to get out of this alive.

“Everyone, fall back!” she yelled, gesturing for the team to retreat to a safer location. “The exit is over there!”

As they made their way towards an exit, they encountered another group of extremists, who was determined to stop them. A fierce firefight broke out once again, with the team fighting for every inch of ground.

Despite their best efforts, the extremists seemed to have the upper hand at the beginning. They had launched a surprise attack that had caught the team off guard, and they were using some of the most advanced weaponry available to them.

After they catch their breath, they continued to push forward step by step, they managed to gain a foothold and take out several of the extremists. The tide of the battle began to turn, and Emma could see that they might just have a chance of making it out alive.

Just as they were about to make a final push towards the exit, they heard another loud explosion from behind them. Emma turned around just in time to see one gunman setting off a bomb that destroyed a portion of the lab.

The shockwave knocked the team off their feet, sending them flying through the air. When Emma looked up, she knew that they needed to get out of there immediately. She struggled to her feet, coughing and gasping for breath as she led her team towards an escape route.

As they burst through the exit door and into the sunlight, Emma caught a glimpse of a figure in the distance, the same guy dressed in black with a weapon at his hands.

"Look out!" Sarah shouted, as she tackled Maria to the ground. A bullet whizzed past them, striking the wall behind them with a loud thud.

The team scrambled to their feet and sprinted towards the parking lot, dodging bullets as they ran. Emma's heart was pounding in her chest as she tried to keep track of everyone, but the chaos of the situation made it difficult. When they approached the lot, Emma saw that several of the team's cars had been destroyed in the attack.

"Split up!" she shouted, her voice barely audible over the gunfire. "We'll meet back at the office in five minutes."

The team scattered, each person taking a different route in an effort to lose their pursuers. Emma ran towards a nearby alleyway, ducking behind a dumpster as she caught her breath. She could hear the sound of footsteps approaching, and she held her breath, praying that they would pass her by.

Suddenly, a figure loomed over her, pointing a gun at her head. Emma froze, her heart pounding in her chest as she stared down the barrel of the gun.

"Hello, Emma," said a voice she didn't recognize.

"Who are you? What do you want?" Emma asked, trying to keep her voice steady.

"I'm Robert. You just need to know that we're here because we want you to stop interfering with our plans," Robert said, a cold smile on his face. "And we'll do whatever it takes to make sure that happens."

Emma's mind raced as she tried to think of a way out of the situation. She knew that the rest of the team was in danger, and she needed to find a way to warn them.

Suddenly, she heard the sound of footsteps approaching from behind Robert. Before he could react, Emma lashed out with a swift kick to his knee, causing him to stumble forward. She grabbed the gun from his hand and turned to face the newcomer.

It was three gunmen. Before Emma could react, one of them had her in a headlock, his arm tight around Emma's throat.

"Let her go!" a voice shouted from behind them. Emma recognized it as Tom's.

The gunman hesitated for a moment, giving Emma the opening she needed. With a swift motion, Emma grabbed a nearby lab stool and swung it at his head, knocking him to the ground. Robert rushed at Emma, but she was ready for him, using her martial arts training to disarm him and pin him to the ground.

Tom and Emma pointed their guns at Robert and his fellows. Other gunmen hesitated, unsure of what to do next. Emma looked at them with a mix of anger and compassion. She knew that they were just pawns in a larger game.

At that moment, the rest of Emma's team regrouped with her and determined to protect themselves. "Who is the one dressed in black? Tell me," Emma demanded.

"He is our leader of this attack, Carlos Fernandez. He is a ruthless fighter with a reputation for taking down his opponents without mercy. He is going to kill you guys," Robert said.

Moments later, they heard a loud banging at the door. A guy in black walked calmly into the lab, a confident smirk on his face. It is Carlos.

"Well, well, well," he said. "It seems like you guys are still alive. I'm impressed."

Emma stepped forward, her eyes locked on Carlos. "Carlos, one of the core members of the Bright Dawn Movement, we're not afraid of you," she said. "We're ready for you now."

Carlos chuckled. "Oh, you know who I'm now," he said. "But let's see if you can back up those words with actions."

23

The Cost of Victory

As they regrouped, John and Mike stepped forward. "We'll take care of Carlos Fernandez," John said, his voice steady.

Emma nodded, knowing that it was a dangerous task. "Be careful," she warned them.

They both assented, and then turned to face Carlos. Both sides immediately returned fire fiercely, but neither could gain the upper hand. Eventually, they ran out of bullets and had to rely on their primitive hand-to-hand combat skills to determine the winner. He was a strong and formidable opponent, but John and Mike were determined to take him down.

The fight was intense, with Carlos unleashing a barrage of kicks and punches using his Muay Thai skills. John was a skilled fighter in his own right, but he struggled to keep up with Carlos's speed and agility. Mike, on the other hand, used his knowledge of microbiology to create a distraction, throwing vials of bacteria at Carlos. The vials shattered on the floor, releasing a cloud of bacteria that momentarily disoriented Carlos.

But Carlos was quick to recover, and he continued his attack on John and Mike. The two men fought bravely, exchanging blows with Carlos, but it was clear that they were outmatched. Carlos was too strong, formidable and skilful, and it seemed like he could anticipate their every move.

John immediately launched an attack, throwing a series of punches and kicks at Carlos. However, Carlos seemed calm and quickly dodged the attacks, using his body skills to counterattack. He struck John's chin with his knee, causing him to lose balance.

Mike quickly jumped into the fight to help John. He tried to kick Carlos' legs, but Carlos easily dodged and seized the opportunity to counterattack. He grabbed Mike's arm and attacked his shoulder joint with his elbow.

John returned to the fight, attempting to use a more strategic approach against Carlos. He used his previous boxing techniques to try to corner Carlos. However, Carlos quickly counterattacked by suppressing John's neck with his leg, rendering him immobile and causing him unconsciousness.

Mike, seeing his friend's defeat, attempted to rush in again to help but Carlos was ready for him. With lightning-quick reflexes, Carlos grabbed Mike's arm, twisted it behind his back and slammed him against the wall. Mike let out a cry of pain as Carlos struck him with several quick blows to his ribs and stomach before launching a powerful knee strike that sent Mike collapsing to the ground.

John, now starting to regain consciousness, attempted to stand up and re-enter the fight, but Carlos was too fast and too skilled. With a swift kick to the side, Carlos knocked John back down to the ground. He then proceeded to land a series of heavy punches and elbow strikes, leaving John gasping for breath.

As John and Mike lay helpless on the ground, Carlos stood over them, triumphant. He looked down at his defeated opponents with contempt, knowing that he had emerged victorious. With one final blow, he dealt a fatal strike that ended the lives of both John and Mike. The room fell silent as Carlos slowly walked away from the scene, leaving behind devastation and sorrow.

The scene is one of tragedy and loss. The two men fell to the ground, their bodies lifeless, there was an eerie silence that descended upon the scene. The other members of their team stood frozen, unable to believe what had just happened.

John's body lay on the ground with his eyes closed, his chest no longer rising and falling with breath. There was blood seeping out from the wound inflicted upon him, staining the pavement beneath him. Mike was lying a few feet away, also motionless, with his eyes open but unseeing. His expression was one of shock and pain, frozen on his face forever.

Emma watched in horror as her colleagues were killed before her eyes. She felt a surge of anger and grief, and she knew that she had to stop Carlos before he could cause any more harm.

As Carlos stood over the fallen bodies of John and Mike, he couldn't help but feel a sense of satisfaction. He had accomplished what he and his group had set out to do – to destroy the work of the rival team and eliminate anyone who got in their way.

But the victory was short-lived as Emma and others emerged from their hiding places, their faces etched with a mixture of fear and determination. They had seen their colleagues fall, and they were not going to let their sacrifice be in vain.

Emma stepped forward, her voice shaking with anger and sadness.

"You may have won this battle, but you haven't won the war," she said, staring directly into Carlos's eyes. "We will not rest until we bring you and your group to justice for what you have done."

Carlos smirked, unimpressed by her words. "Hahaha! You may try, but you won't succeed," he replied, his voice dripping with arrogance. "We are willing to do whatever it takes to achieve our goals, even if it means sacrificing ourselves."

Emma's team members exchanged worried glances. They knew they were up against a dangerous and determined enemy, but they also knew that they couldn't give up without a fight.

Suddenly, there was a loud explosion, and the room shook violently. Carlos stumbled back and his head hit the wall, momentarily disoriented, losing his balance and falling onto the ground with protruding iron rods. The sharp rods pierced his body, causing him to spit blood and immobilizing him.

When the dust settled, Emma approached Carlos on the ground. "It's over," she said, her voice firm but tinged with sadness. "You've lost."

Carlos looked up at her, his eyes filled with hatred and desperation. "You may have defeated us, but you haven't won. Virus saves the world," he spat, before taking his last breath and passing away.

Emma and her team stood in silence, taking in the devastation that surrounded them. They had won the battle, but at a great cost – John and Mike.

24

The Goals

The team was shaken by the recent attack on their lab. They had lost John and Mike, two valued members of the team. After a day of sorrow, the team was determined to find out what ultimate goal of the Bright Dawn Movement was. They knew that they couldn't let the group succeed in their plans.

After securing the area and ensuring that there were no other threats, the team began to search the bodies of the attackers. They found weapons, explosives, and other tools of destruction. As they searched Carlos's body, Laura noticed a small device that looked like a USB drive.

"Hey, guys, I found something," Laura called out to her team. They gathered around as Laura held up the device.

"It looks like a USB drive," Sarah observed.

Emma nodded. "Let's take it back to the lab and see what's on it."

Back in the lab, Daniel sat at his desk, staring intently at the USB drive in front of him for a moment. Then he plugged the device into a computer and began to search through the files.

"It's password protected," Daniel said. "Alright team, we need to crack this password-protected USB drive as soon as possible," he said, addressing his colleagues.

"Okay, let's get started," said Maria. "I'll try to brute force it using a dictionary attack[2] first."

"That might take too long," said Daniel, "We need to explore other options."

"I can try to exploit any vulnerabilities in the encryption algorithm that was used," Sarah offered.

Daniel meditated. "That could work, but we don't have much time. We need to find the best computer engineers in the world to help us crack this."

They contacted Director Johnson from the Department of Homeland Security. By this help, they finally found a team of experts who were willing to take on the challenge.

"Hello, I'm Emma. Thank you for agreeing to help," Emma greeted the team of experts over video call.

"No problem," said Tim Osher the team leader, "We hope to start now. Can you send me the encrypted file?"

Emma shared the file with the team and they immediately got to work.

"This is tough," said one of the experts, "The encryption is top-level. We're going to have to use some advanced techniques."

Over the next few hours, Emma and Daniel watched as the experts worked their magic. They tried everything from sophisticated algorithms to social engineering tactics.

---

[2] A dictionary attack is a method used in cryptanalysis and computer security, where an attacker uses a limited set of possible passwords or keys to break a cipher or authentication mechanism.

Finally, after what seemed like an eternity, Tim exclaimed, "I've got it!"

Daniel breathed a huge sigh of relief. "Thank you so much. You guys are amazing!"

"It was our pleasure," said Tim, "Glad we could be of help."

After a few more hours of searching., Emma found some important documents outlining the plans of the Bright Dawn Movement.

"Guys, you need to see this," Emma said, turning to her team.

Emma briefed the team on her findings, and everyone huddled around the computer screen. She revealed that the Bright Dawn Movement had nefarious plans to exploit the pandemic for their own gain – **they created chaos, fear, disorder and panic to claim power and control over the United States**.

"They were using the pandemic as a cover," Maria said, her voice filled with disgust. "They didn't care about the lives that were being lost. They just saw it as an opportunity to further their own agenda."

The team was stunned by the revelation. They had suspected that the group had a larger goal in mind, but they had never imagined that it would be so sinister.

"What is their exact plan to claim power and control over the US?" Tom inquired.

"We have to figure it out and stop them," Maria said, her jaw clenched in anger.

"We will," Emma replied, her voice firm. "We'll use every resource we have to bring them down."

The team spent the rest of the day analyzing the documents and gathering more information about the Bright Dawn Movement. They knew that they were up against a dangerous enemy, but they were determined to stop them at all costs.

Their hearts were heavy as they tried to process the loss of her colleagues. They felt a deep sense of sadness and grief that weighed heavily on their souls. They couldn't help but think about the families of John and Mike, and the pain they must be feeling.

At the same time, Emma also felt a sense of determination growing within her. She knew that she couldn't let her emotions get in the way of the task at hand. John and Mike had made the ultimate sacrifice, and it was up to her and the rest of the team to carry on their legacy.

When the hours ticked by, Emma's emotions continued to shift. She went from feeling overwhelmed with grief to feeling a sense of anger and frustration towards the Bright Dawn Movement. She couldn't believe that anyone could be so callous and selfish to use a pandemic for their own gain.

Emma took a deep breath and closed her eyes, trying to calm the turmoil of emotions that were churning inside her.

"I can't let my feelings get in the way," she said to herself. "I need to stay focused on the task at hand."

Ten minutes later, she opened her eyes again and reminded herself of the importance of remaining clear-headed.

"Emma Lee, you have to be rational and objective," she continued to say to herself. "Your priority is to stop Gabriel's plans and save innocent lives."

Emma was determined to leave no stone unturned in her efforts to put an end to the group's destructive agenda.

"We'll use all available resources," she thought, "to track them down and prevent any more harm from being done."

25

A Response Plan

They worked tirelessly for days, analyzing data, conducting experiments, and coming up with a comprehensive report on the Bright Dawn Movement's plans. The report detailed the group's motive and potential impact on the US if they were to succeed.

Finally, the report was ready to be sent to the United Nations (UN), the WHO and the US government. Emma gathered her team in the conference room and began to present their findings.

"As you all know, Gabriel had a motive beyond just causing chaos and destruction," Emma said, projecting the report onto the screen. "They intend to use the pandemic to achieve their own goals, and those goals are nothing short of catastrophic."

The team listened in silence as Emma went through the report, detailing the group's plans to weaponize Virocide X and release it on a global scale. She showed them the data they had collected, the experiments they had conducted, and the evidence they had gathered from Carlos and his group.

"This is a definitely dire situation, and we cannot underestimate the danger this group poses to the world," Emma continued. "We need to send this report to the UN, the WHO and the US government immediately, and we need to do everything in our power to stop this group from carrying out their plans."

The team nodded in agreement, and Emma quickly drafted a message to the UN, the WHO and the US government, attaching the report as evidence. She explained the urgency of the situation and urged them to take immediate action.

As Emma and her team gathered together, they discussed their next steps. They had uncovered parts of the plan of the extremist group, but they needed to act fast to stop them from succeeding. Emma led the discussion, asking for input from everyone.

After a few moments of brainstorming, they came up with a list of strategies. They would continue to work on developing a vaccine that could counteract the effects of Virocide X. They would also reach out to other labs and experts in the field, seeking collaboration and support in their efforts.

Additionally, they decided to create a public awareness campaign to inform people about the danger of the extremist group's plans and the importance of taking necessary precautions. They would also coordinate with government agencies and law enforcement to increase security measures and prevent any further attacks.

Finally, they delved into the correlation between Virocide X and Gabriel's ways of obtaining power and control over the US government. Subsequently, they had to formulate a plan to thwart his efforts.

As the meeting came to a close, Emma summarized the strategies they had come up with and assigned tasks to each of them. They knew it was going to be a difficult road ahead, but they were determined to succeed.

Emma and Sarah were responsible for the last task. Sarah sat at her desk, staring blankly at the computer screen in front of her. She had been searching for any information that could help her and the team track down Gabriel and his followers, but so far she had come up empty-handed.

Just as she was about to give up for the day, her smart phone rang. "Hello?" she answered, hoping it was good news.

"Sarah, this is Dr. Croll," a friendly voice said on the other end. "I have some information that might be of interest to you."

Sarah sat up straighter in her chair, feeling a flicker of hope. "What kind of information?"

"Well, I did some more research on the nanobot that we found inside Maya's body," Dr. Croll said. "And I think I may have found a lead."

Sarah leaned forward, her heart racing. "Tell me more."

"It seems that the nanobot was ordered by a global investment company called GoldRock Capital," Dr. Croll replied. "I did some digging, and I found out that the founder and CEO of the company is a man named Alexander Stone."

Sarah scribbled down the name, feeling a surge of excitement. "Do you know anything else about him?"

"Yes, actually," Dr. Croll replied. "He's a very wealthy and powerful man, with connections all over the world. He's rumored to be involved in some pretty shady business deals, so it wouldn't surprise me if he had something to do with Gabriel and his plans."

Sarah thanked Dr. Croll for the information and hung up, feeling energized by the new lead. She knew that GoldRock Capital could be the key to unlocking Gabriel's plans and stopping him once and for all.

She immediately contacted the rest of the team, briefing them on the latest development. They quickly got to work, researching everything they could find on Alexander Stone and GoldRock Capital. They discovered that the company had its headquarters in the heart of New York City, and that Stone was known for his extravagant lifestyle and ruthless business tactics.

26

Alexander Stone's Hidden Lair

Emma and Sarah returned to New York City for Alexander Stone.

They had been monitoring Alexander Stone for weeks, trying to gather as much information as possible. They had discovered that he often went to his personal villa in the suburbs of New York City every weekend.

They decided to do a stakeout to gather more information. One weekend, they hid in a nearby forest and set up surveillance equipment to monitor Alexander's movements. As expected, Alexander arrived at his villa on Friday evening. The team watched as he spent the day relaxing by the pool and entertaining guests. But then, on Saturday night, something strange happened. Alexander stayed at the garage overnight.

"Is there a way for us to observe what he did inside the garage?" Emma inquired.

Sarah remembered a new technology that had recently been developed. "I have an idea. We could use the Ground-Penetrating Radar (GPR) with advanced imaging technology that I saw at the Washington lab last month."

Emma looked at Sarah in surprise. "What kind of technology are you talking about?" asked Emma.

"GPR is a non-destructive imaging technique that uses high-frequency electromagnetic waves to generate images of subsurface structures. The advantages of it for scanning the inside structure of a garage include its non-destructive nature, high resolution, and ability to detect different materials, such as wood, metal, and plastic." Sarah explained.

"How does it work?" Emma inquired, expressing her interest.

"The GPR system typically consists of three very tiny main components: the antenna, the control unit, and the display unit. The antenna is responsible for transmitting and receiving the electromagnetic waves. The control unit generates the signals and controls the timing of the measurements. The display unit shows the results of the scan in real-time and allows for data processing and analysis," Sarah explained.

"Sounds promising," said Emma. "But how do we get the components close enough to the garage without alerting people inside the villa?"

"We could use a remote control device to operate a BeeWatch and retrieve the components from a safe distance, which would help us avoid detection," Sarah proposed.

They quickly put the plan into action. They contacted the lab and requested the GPR system and a few BeeWatchs, which were delivered within hours. They carefully programmed the bees' flight path, making sure to avoid detection by any potential enemies. The garage was monitored by the GPR, allowing them to track Alexander's every movement inside. Within a few minutes, Alexander turned a candle holder on the wall, revealing a hidden entrance to a basement as the wall slid back.

"This is it," Emma said, her eyes widening with realization. "He is hiding something. This is probably where Gabriel is planning to launch his attack."

"Later tonight after he leaves, we should go inside and inspect it," Sarah suggested.

Emma agreed.

Around 5:30 am, Alexander left his garage and returned to his villa. Shortly after, Emma and Sarah sneaked into the garage, rotated the candle holder on the wall, which caused the passage to the basement to open. Slowly, they walked down the stairs into the basement. The lighting system on either side of the passage immediately activated, revealing a startling sight before them. The basement was filled with advanced technology, including computer servers, tablets, laboratory equipment, and even some AI robots. The desk was cluttered with disorganized papers, and a large map hung on the wall, dotted with pushpins and marked with arrows of various colors and sizes. Written in the bottom right corner was "Patagonia, Argentina".

"Patagonia. Unbelievable," Emma muttered.

"Is that a place?" Sarah inquired.

"I know this place. Patagonia is a vast and desolate region in the southern part of Argentina, including the western Andes Mountains and the eastern coast of the continent. This area has extreme, unpredictable weather conditions and rugged terrain, so it is a tough location to navigate. Gabriel may hide there." Emma explained.

Emma and Sarah quickly took photos and gathered as much evidence as possible before slipping out of the basement undetected.

27

Gabriel's Ultimate Ruse

The team gathered again and read what Emma and Sarah discovered. They had discovered crucial information regarding Gabriel's plan from a report. Gabriel's plan began in 2067, one year before the presidential election year in the United States, where his extremist organization unleashed the deadly virus Virocide X. This caused widespread death and social unrest, and posed a serious threat to the existing government's power. However, Gabriel had a solution to the virus, which he revealed as the second step in his plan. At 9:00 am on 1st November, he planned to announce the availability of the solution and necessary protective measures through live stream, which won not only wealth but also the trust and support of the people. Ultimately, Gabriel's actions led to his successful election as the coming US president in 2068, the seizure of power, and a new era for the country.

Laura expressed her resentment. "He is a crazy man. We have to stop his announcement! We can't let him get the public's attention."

Sarah agreed and added. "His insane plan needs to be halted immediately. Additionally, we must acquire the solution he possesses to cure the infected individuals as soon as possible. Too many people have died due to this outbreak. We need to find him," she said with anger.

"What day is it today?" Daniel asked.

"Time is short, let's take action," Emma said, stating that it was the 26th of October.

With knowledge of Gabriel's entire plan, the team was determined to prevent it. However, they knew that they had to proceed with care and caution as even the slightest mistake could alert Gabriel and his organization, putting their mission at risk. The stakes were high, and the team understood the gravity of the situation. They meticulously planned every move, taking into account all possible scenarios and contingencies.

Daniel said. "I have an idea. We can send a thousand BeeWatches equipped with the cutting-edge GPS tracking system and advanced imaging technology over the area of Patagonia. It can provide high-resolution images and can even detect heat signatures. I believe that we might be able to see if there's any activity in the area in three to four days."

Emma spoke up. "We could also use our contacts in Argentina to gather intel on the Gabriel's base. We have friends in the local government who could help us obtain information on the base's location and any recent activity in the area."

Maria suggested. "If we have the exact location information, we could go to the base ourselves."

Tom raised his hand. "I think we need to consider the risks of each plan. The GPS tracking system plan could be dangerous if the extremist group detects the BeeWatches. The second plan could take time, and we might not have that much time."

Emma agreed, "Yes, and we also need to consider the risk of going to the base ourselves. We could be outnumbered, and we don't know their weapons capability."

Maria chimed in. "But if we don't go, then we risk letting them carry out their plan, which could have catastrophic consequences."

Laura spoke up. "I agree with Maria. We cannot let them succeed, and going to the base might be the only option we have left."

Sarah looked at everyone. "But what if we get caught or worse, killed? We are not equipped to handle a situation like that."

Maria put her hand on Sarah's shoulder, "We have to be brave, Sarah. Our mission is to protect as many lives as we can, and we can't do that by being afraid."

Emma turned to the group. "Let's make a list of the risks and benefits of each plan, and then vote on which one we should pursue."

They all agreed and started to brainstorm the risks and benefits of each plan.

Tom spoke up. "Plan A, the GPS tracking system, has the benefit of being remote, but the downside is that it could be detected by the extremist group. Plan B, the backup plan, could take too long, and we might not have that much time. But Plan C, going to the base ourselves, has the benefit of being the most direct approach, but the risk is too high."

Maria said. "But if we go to the base ourselves, we could get a better sense of what we're dealing with and plan accordingly."

Emma added. "And we can't just sit and wait for the extremist group to carry out their plan. We have to be proactive and take action."

Sarah said worriedly. "But what about the risk of getting caught or killed?"

Laura spoke up. "We will take all necessary precautions, and we have trained for situations like this. We will be careful and stay alert."

The discussion came to a halt for a moment as everyone reconsidered. Ten minutes later.

Tom proposed. "Okay, I suggest we can come up with a new plan that combines Plan A and Plan C. We'll use the GPS tracking system, but replace the thousand BeeWatches with only several drones for safety."

Daniel asked. "But won't the drones also be detected by the extremist group?"

Tom clarified. "It's not necessary. Drones have a much higher altitude and more powerful scanning capabilities than BeeWatches, which makes them difficult to detect. Besides, we can program them to fly erratically, making it even more challenging for the enemy to track."

Sarah asked. "What about the risk of going to the base ourselves? Won't that still be too high?"

Tom said. "Yes, it will be risky, but we can minimize the danger by moving quickly and stay on high alert. I believe this is our best option."

Maria asked. "What about the backup plan? Shouldn't we still have one?"

Emma spoke up. "Absolutely. Plan B will be our backup, just in case something goes wrong with Plan A and C. We can't afford to take any chances."

Daniel nodded. "Okay, so the new plan is to use the GPS tracking system with drones instead of BeeWatches, and we go to Patagonia ourselves at the same time while keeping Plan B as our backup?"

Tom said. "Yes, that's right. Let's get to work and make this happen."

Emma continued. "Let's get ready, everyone. We have a difficult task ahead of us."

They all got up from the table, ready to face the challenges ahead.

As they were leaving the room, Daniel stopped Sarah and whispered. "Don't worry, Sarah. We'll make sure you stay safe."

Sarah smiled, feeling reassured by Daniel's words.

They all began to prepare for their mission, gathering their gear and reviewing their plan of attack. They knew the risks were high, but they were determined to stop the Gabriel's plan at all costs.

28

Across the Wilderness in Patagonia

The team set out on their journey to Patagonia, aware of the harsh weather conditions and difficult terrain that lay ahead. They packed their bags with all the necessary equipment, including warm clothing, hiking boots, climbing gear, and powerful weapon.

The US government, with UN coordination, received authorization from the Argentine government to use unmanned surveillance drones for detecting activities in their airspace. Consequently, Mr. Carl, the Director of the Department of Homeland Security, initiated Plan A as the team flew to Bariloche airport in Argentina. In the afternoon of 29th October, just after three days of investigation, Carl delivered positive news to the team, noting that they had detected some irregular human activities near Maquinchao and forwarding the coordinates to Emma.

After they dot the coordinates, they traveled deeper into the wilderness, the terrain became increasingly treacherous. The path was steep and rocky, and the air grew colder and thinner with every step. The team struggled to keep their balance on the uneven ground, and the weight of their backpacks made their progress slow and arduous.

Emma's glasses fogged up as she trudged through the dense fog that surrounded them. She wiped them with her sleeve, trying to get a better view of their surroundings. "This weather is really making it hard to see anything," she muttered to himself.

Maria was struggling to catch her breath as they climbed higher. She paused to take a few deep breaths before resuming her climb. “I didn’t expect it to be this difficult,” she said, panting.

Laura stumbled on a loose rock and nearly fell. Tom quickly steadied her. “Be careful,” he warned her. “We can’t afford any injuries out here.”

They continued on, facing one obstacle after another. They had to cross a raging river, climb over boulders, and navigate through dense grassland. The weather was unforgiving, with strong winds and hailstones pelting down on them.

Sarah slipped on a patch of wet rocks and fell, hitting her head on the ground. Daniel quickly rushed to her side to check for any injuries. “Are you okay?” he asked, concerned.

Sarah shook her head, trying to clear the dizziness. “I think I hit my head, but it wasn’t severe,” she said, groaning. “But I’ll be fine.”

Tom scanned the surroundings, looking for any signs of danger. He had his hand on his gun, ready to defend his team if necessary. “We need to stay alert,” he reminded them. “We don’t know what kind of wildlife or other dangers we might encounter out here.”

Despite the challenges, the team continued on, determined to reach their destination. They pushed through the harsh weather conditions and difficult terrain, relying on their training and expertise to navigate through the wilderness.

Hours passed as they climbed higher and higher up the mountain. The air grew thinner, and their progress became even slower. But finally, they reached the top, and a breathtaking view opened up before them.

Emma took a deep breath of the fresh mountain air, feeling invigorated by the journey. "It's beautiful up here," she said, looking out at the view.

Maria nodded in agreement. "It's amazing what we can achieve when we work together," she said, smiling at her teammates.

Laura took out her smart phone and snapped a few photos of the view. "This will make a great addition to my collection," she said, grinning.

The team rested for a few minutes, enjoying the view and catching their breath. But they knew they couldn't stay there for long. The base was still a long way off, and there were more challenges to come.

They continued on, carefully picking their way through the harsh terrain. They navigated through thick forests and treacherous bogs, constantly checking their map and compass to ensure they were on the right track. The weather was unforgiving, with strong winds and sudden downpours making their journey even more difficult.

As they descended the mountain, they encountered an unexpected obstacle: a raging river that blocked their path. The water was murky and swift, making it impossible to wade across. They searched for a safe crossing point but found none.

"We're going to have to build a bridge," said Emma, examining the river.

"Out of what?" asked Sarah, looking around at the sparse vegetation.

"Logs," replied Emma. "We'll have to find some trees that we can cut down and use to build a bridge."

Without choices, they spent several hours searching for suitable trees, finally finding a stand of tall pines that looked sturdy enough. With Tom's help, they used their machetes to chop down several trees and began the arduous task of lugging them to the riverbank.

It was slow going, but they were determined. They worked in teams, using ropes to drag the logs into place and secure them to the opposite bank. Maria and Sarah kept watch, scanning the area for any signs of danger.

Finally, after several hours of hard work, the bridge was complete. They crossed over one by one, grateful to be on the other side of the river.

"That was intense," said Daniel, wiping sweat from his forehead.

"We've still got a long way to go," reminded Tom, checking the map. "We need to keep moving."

They continued on, their progress slowed by the difficult terrain. They climbed steep hills and scrambled over jagged rocks, taking care not to slip and fall. The weather didn't let up, with strong gusts of wind threatening to knock them off their feet.

After what felt like hours, they finally reached the base of the mountain. They paused to catch their breath, taking in the breathtaking view of the valley below.

"That's where we're headed," said Emma, pointing to a small dilapidated wooden cabin in the middle of a grassland. "The extremist group's base is located there."

"How are we supposed to get across? There's a river ahead of us," asked Sarah, eyeing the swift current.

"We'll have to build another bridge," replied Tom, studying the map.

"But we don't have any more logs," said Maria.

"We'll have to find another way," said Tom, his eyes scanning the area.

They searched for a few hours, but found no suitable crossing point. The river was too wide and deep, with no sign of any other way across.

"We're going to have to swim," said Daniel, his tone grim.

"Swim? Are you kidding me?" repeated Sarah, her eyes widening.

"It's the only way," said Daniel. "We'll have to swim across with our gear and hope for the best. No time for another bridge."

They stripped down to their underwear, packing their clothes and equipment into waterproof bags. Daniel, who was a strong swimmer, took the lead. They formed a human chain, linking arms and wading into the frigid water.

The current was stronger than they had anticipated, pulling them downstream and making it difficult to stay together. Maria and Sarah struggled to keep up, their legs growing numb from the cold.

"Just a little farther," encouraged Emma, her voice barely audible over the roar of the river.

They finally reached the opposite bank, shivering and exhausted. They quickly dressed and set up camp, huddling together for warmth. The weather had taken a turn for the worse, with a sudden snowstorm.

It was 9:00 am on 30th October, 24 hours left for Gabriel's broadcasting.

29

Obstacle After Obstacle

It was 4:00 pm on 30th June, the team approached the proposed route to the small dilapidated wooden cabin of a grassland. However, they were met with a roadblock consisting of large boulders and tree trunks that had been intentionally placed to impede any passing vehicles. Tom immediately suspected Gabriel's group and signaled the team to halt.

"We need to find another way," Tom said, scanning the area for any signs of danger.

"But we don't have much time. We need to reach the cabin before they can launch their attack," Daniel added.

They began to survey the surrounding terrain for any possible detours, but the rocky terrain made it difficult to find a viable path. Suddenly, they heard the sound of approaching vehicles, and their hearts raced with anxiety.

"Quick, hide!" Tom ordered, and the team scattered behind nearby boulders and trees.

Two pickup trucks, each carrying several heavily armed men, appeared around the corner and stopped in front of the roadblock. The men quickly jumped out of their vehicles and began inspecting the area, checking for any signs of intruders.

The team held their breath, hoping to avoid detection. However, one of the men noticed a footprint near one of the boulders and raised the alarm.

"We've got company!" he shouted, and the other men quickly sprang into action.

The team realized that they had been discovered and quickly drew their weapons. They saw several gunmen rushing towards them, shouting and firing their weapons. Emma and her fellows quickly drew their own weapons and took cover behind nearby rocks and trees.

The air was filled with the smell and sound of gunfire, with bullets whizzing past their ears and hitting the ground around them. Emma could feel her heart pounding in her chest as she tried to steady her aim and return fire. She heard her teammates shouting out position updates and warnings, trying to coordinate their movements and keep each other safe.

Despite being outnumbered, the team managed to hold their ground and fend off the attackers. They fired back with calculated precision, taking down enemy after enemy. They used cover effectively, moving from place to place to avoid getting hit. They also used smoke grenades and flashbangs to distract and disorient the attackers, giving them an advantage in the fight.

As the gunfight continued, Emma noticed that her fellows were starting to tire. They had been on the move for days along the way. Their wounds and exhaustion were starting to take a toll.

But despite their weariness, they continued to fight with determination and grit, their eyes fixed on the goal of stopping Gabriel. Finally, after several minutes of intense fighting, the last of the gunmen lay motionless on the ground. The team members looked around, panting and sweating from the exertion. They checked on each other's injuries, administering first aid where necessary. Though victorious, the team members were left wounded and exhausted by the intense gunfight.

"We need to keep moving," Daniel urged, helping one of the injured team members to stand up.

"Agreed," Tom said, checking the map once more. "We'll have to take a longer route, but it should lead us to the cabin safely."

Their journey was arduous and perilous, as they navigated through treacherous rivers and thick forests that impeded their progress. As the team journeyed through the Patagonia wilderness, they encountered a variety of obstacles, including challenging terrain and unexpected wildlife encounters. One of the most daunting predators they faced was the puma, also known as the Mountain Lion.

Pumas are one of the largest carnivores in Patagonia, capable of taking down prey much larger than themselves. As the team traveled through the rugged terrain, they remained vigilant for signs of puma activity, knowing that an encounter with one of these powerful predators could be deadly.

Despite their caution, they did come face to face with a puma on one occasion. They had been navigating through a rocky gorge when they spotted movement up ahead. At first, they thought it might be a deer or another herbivore, but then the animal moved into view and they realized it was a puma.

The predator was crouched low to the ground, its muscles tense and ready to pounce. The team froze in place, knowing that any sudden movements could trigger an attack. They slowly backed away, keeping their eyes locked on the puma's every move.

Emma's heart was pounding in her chest as she watched its every move. She knew that they needed to act fast if they were going to survive this encounter. Emma signaled to the team, and they slowly reached for their weapons, never taking their eyes off the predator.

With a fierce growl, the puma lunged forward, its claws outstretched. The team sprang into action, firing a volley of shots at the charging animal. The puma was hit but still managed to land on Daniel, knocking him to the ground. Maria didn't hesitate. She rushed forward and swung her machete at the puma, striking it squarely in the head. The predator let out a ferocious roar before collapsing to the ground, lifeless.

The team cheered in victory, but they knew that they needed to be cautious, as there could be more dangers lurking in the wilderness. The team continued on their journey, now even more aware of the dangers lurking in the wilderness. Encounters like this were a reminder of just how unpredictable and dangerous the Patagonia wilderness could be. However, they persevered, using their training and experience to stay alert and avoid further dangers as they pushed forward towards their goal.

Finally, the team arrived at the entrance of the cabin they had been searching for. They could see the fortified walls and security measures designed to keep intruders out. However, to their surprise, no battle ensued upon their arrival. The silence was eerie, and they wondered what could be going on behind those walls. The team remained on high alert, scanning their surroundings for any sign of danger.

It was 8:30 am on 1st November, 30 minutes left for Gabriel's broadcasting.

30

Rachel Winters

As the team cautiously entered the cabin, they were struck by the eerie silence that enveloped them. They knew that Gabriel's group was preparing for another action, and yet there was no sign of any activity. The team scanned their surroundings, looking for any clues that would lead them to Gabriel and his followers.

As they searched the cabin, they stumbled upon a hidden underground passage. It was well-concealed, and if not for Daniel's sharp eyes, they might have missed it entirely. The team looked at each other, realizing that this could be their only chance to catch Gabriel before it was too late.

"We need to check this out," Tom said, gesturing towards the entrance to the underground passage.

"Agreed," Emma said, nodding. "But we need to be careful. We don't know what we're walking into."

They descended into the underground passage slowly, their weapons drawn and ready for anything that might come their way. As they made their way through the winding tunnels, they could hear the sounds of footsteps echoing off the walls.

Suddenly, they heard a voice calling out from the darkness. "Emma? Is that you?" Emma recognized the voice almost immediately. It was Rachel Winters. She was surprised to see her old friend among Gabriel's followers, and she felt a sense of sadness wash over her.

"Rachel, what are you doing here?" Emma asked, her weapon trained on Rachel.

"I'm sorry, Emma," Rachel replied, her voice trembling. "But I believe in Gabriel's vision: **Virus saves the world**. He has a plan to save humanity from itself, and I want to be a part of it."

Emma shook her head, feeling a mix of anger and disappointment. "How could you betray humans like this, Rachel? We were friends once," she said, stepping forward cautiously. "Rachel, we need to stop Gabriel before he hurts anyone else."

Rachel stepped out of the shadows, her hands raised her weapon. "I know, Emma, but I can't let you do that. Gabriel is my leader, my faith, and I will defend him with my life."

"Rachel, please," Emma pleaded. "We don't want to hurt you. Just help us stop Gabriel."

Rachel looked down at the ground, unable to meet Emma's gaze. "I know, Emma. But I can't just sit back and watch as the world falls apart. They're polluting the planet, destroying the environment, and causing chaos. Gabriel's plan is the only hope we have. His plan was to cleanse everything."

"Rachel, please," Emma pleaded again. "You don't have to do this. There's still time for you to come back to us."

Rachel just shook her head, looking at Emma with a mixture of sadness and determination. "I'm sorry, Emma. But I can't abandon my beliefs. Gabriel's vision is the only hope we have. You don't understand…"

The tension in the air was palpable as the two groups faced off against each other. Suddenly, the peace was shattered as the sound of gunfire echoed through the tunnels. The two groups clashed, firing their weapons and engaging in fierce hand-to-hand combat.

Emma found herself face to face with Rachel, struggling to fend off her frenzied attacks. She tried to reason with her old friend, urging her to give up and join their cause. But Rachel was beyond reason, her eyes filled with a fanatical zeal as she fought to protect Gabriel.

"Why are you doing this, Rachel?" Emma shouted, trying to be heard over the sounds of gunfire.

"I can't abandon Gabriel's plan," Rachel replied, her voice strained. "He's everything to us. He gave me purpose when I had none."

"You have us," Emma said, gesturing towards the rest of her team. "We're your friends. We care about you."

Rachel hesitated for a moment, her gun lowered slightly. "I know you do, Emma. But my loyalty lies with Gabriel."

The battle continued to rage on, with neither side gaining the upper hand. Although Emma's team was outnumbered and outgunned, they fought with all their might, taking down the enemy one by one.

In the midst of the chaos, Emma saw Rachel fall to the ground, clutching her chest. She rushed over to her old friend, tears streaming down her face. "Rachel, please, don't die," she pleaded.

Rachel looked up at Emma, a faint smile on her lips. "I'm sorry, Emma," she gasped. Emma watched in horror as Rachel's life slipped away in her arms. Despite Emma's best efforts, the fight ended in tragedy and she was left to mourn the loss of her friend.

One minute had passed, Emma couldn't help but think of all the memories she had shared with Rachel. They had met in college, both studying biology. They had bonded over their mutual love of science and their desire to make a difference in the world. Over the years, they had stayed in touch, sharing their successes and failures, their triumphs and struggles. They had even talked about working together one day, using their knowledge to create a better world. But now, those dreams were shattered, replaced by the harsh reality of Gabriel's twisted vision. Emma knew that she would never be able to forget Rachel and the sacrifices she had made for a cause she believed in.

It was 8:50 am on 1st November, 10 minutes left for Gabriel's live steaming.

31

The Final Round

The team had 10 minutes only.

They moved quickly, going through the underground passage room by room, searching for any sign of Gabriel or his followers. They were met with resistance at every turn, but they fought on, determined to put an end to Gabriel's plan once and for all.

The team discovered two Gabriel's followers in a room, preparing explosives to block their path. Without hesitation, the team engaged them in combat. The fight was intense, but they were able to subdue the attackers and disarm the explosives.

"What's our next move?" Daniel asked, looking around the room for any clues.

"We need to find Gabriel," Emma said, scanning the area too. "He's the only one who knows the full extent of his plan."

Just then, they heard a sound coming from a nearby hallway. Emma motioned for her team to follow her, and they moved cautiously towards the source of the noise. Rounding the corner, they arrived in the central area where they encountered a man in his mid-40s with dark hair and piercing blue eyes. He was dressed in a black suit and sitting in front of a tablet. Four burly men with weapons stood nervously on either side of him. As soon as they saw Emma's team, they pointed the guns at them and fired. The team reacted quickly, diving behind cover to evade the attack.

"Who are you?" Maria asked.

"I am Gabriel," declared the man, "the one you have been searching for."

"You're too late, Emma," Gabriel continued. "My plan is already in motion. There's nothing you can do to stop it."

"We know you have a cure. Where is it?" Daniel asked.

"Hahaha! My plan is about to come to fruition, I'm not afraid to tell you. The synthesis method for Virocide X, the antiviral agent, is in the computer system behind me," Gabriel said.

"It was 8:55 am. We don't have time. We should fight directly," Tom suggested.

The team sprang into action, taking cover and returning fire at Gabriel's men. The fight was fierce, with bullets flying in every direction. Emma, Daniel and Sarah worked together to take down the first two attackers, while Maria, Laura and Tom focused on the other two. It was a hard fight. They managed to take them down one by one, but not without casualties. In the midst of the chaos, Laura was hit by a bullet and fell to the ground.

Emma, Daniel and Sarah rushed over to her side, trying to stop the bleeding. "Stay with us, Laura," they pleaded.

It was too late, Laura was badly wounded, blood pouring from a deep gash in her side. She smiled weakly up at Emma, Daniel, Maria, Tom and Sarah.

"Go on without me," she said. "You need to stop Gabriel."

Emma nodded, tears streaming down her face. "We will. I promise."

Laura took her last breath at 8:58 am.

With the immediate threat neutralized, the team turned their attention to Gabriel. With precision, Sarah's shot hit Gabriel square in the chest. The impact caused him to stumble and drop his weapon before collapsing to the ground, struggling for breath. Tom rushed forward, his weapon trained on him.

"You're done, Gabriel," he said, handcuffing him. "It's over." They disarmed him and shut down the live stream at precisely 8:59 am. Just when everyone thought they could finally breathe a sigh of relief, there was a sudden piercing alarm in the room, followed by a voice broadcasting,

"The quantum bomb has been activated. It will detonate in 15 minutes. All personnel please evacuate the base immediately."

Gabriel just sneered at Emma, a look of defiance on her face. "You may have won the battle, but the war is far from over. The countdown has already started because the live streaming stops. My quantum bomb will detonate and destroy everything in its path. The cure for Virocide X is gone forever. Hahaha…"

Gabriel's life came to an end after his final conversation.

"We need to find a way to stop that bomb," Emma said, her voice urgent. The team knew they had to act fast.

"I've tried cutting the power supply, but it's not working. The bomb seems to have its own backup system," Daniel replied.

"I've tried manually disarming it, but the controls are locked out. We need some kind of code or password," Maria explained.

"The quantum bomb has been activated. It will detonate in 10 minutes. All personnel please evacuate the base immediately."

They were running out of time, and panic was starting to set in. Just then, Tom spoke up. "Wait a minute, guys. I remember something." He reached into his bag and pulled out a small robot with blinking lights.

"What is that?" Maria asked.

"It's called Albert, a hacker robot my university colleagues developed with latest AI technology," Tom explained. "It's designed to learn how to hack into any computer system."

Emma's eyes lit up. "That could be our ticket out of here. Can it stop the bomb?"

"I believe so," Tom replied. "The robot can use the power of AI to analyze Gabriel's code and find a way to disable the bomb by hacking into Gabriel's system."

Without wasting a moment, they activated the robot and connected it to the system. Within seconds, the robot was hard at work, analyzing every line of code and searching for vulnerabilities.

As they watched anxiously, the robot suddenly stopped. "I found it!" Tom exclaimed. "There's a backdoor in Gabriel's code. It's hidden, but Albert was able to locate it."

"Do it now! We have only 1 minute left," Sarah shouted.

With trembling hands, they typed in the backdoor code, and to their relief, the bomb's countdown timer stopped ticking away. They had done it.

But they weren't finished yet. They needed to find the cure for Virocide X before it was too late. Thanks to Albert's AI power, they were able to access Gabriel's computer system and extract the information they needed.

Finally, after what felt like hours of searching, Tom let out a triumphant cry. "I found it! The data is here!"

Maria rushed over to him, taking the tablet from his hand. She quickly scanned through the information, hoping that they had found the cure they needed.

"Yes! This is it!" Maria exclaimed, holding up the tablet triumphantly. "We have the cure!"

It was 9:30 am on 1st November, every member breathed a sigh of relief. They had won the war, and they had found the cure for Virocide X. With the cure in hand, they could finally begin to heal the world. But it had come at a great cost. Laura had given her life, and the team would never forget her sacrifice.

32

The Endgame

Emma and Daniel were analyzing the data and cure they had obtained from Gabriel's computer system. After hours of poring over the information, they finally made a breakthrough. They discovered that the virus was a special type of RNA virus that replicated itself by hijacking the host's cells.

"Here is the right cure to stop the virus from replicating," Daniel said, pointing to a graph on the computer screen.

Emma nodded, her eyes fixed on the screen. "But how do we do that?"

"We can target this particular RNA polymerase," Daniel replied. "It's the enzyme that the virus uses to replicate its RNA. If we can inhibit its activity, we can stop the virus from replicating and spreading."

Emma's eyes widened. "That's brilliant. But how do we inhibit its activity?"

"We can try to use a small molecule inhibitor," Daniel said. "It's a chemical compound that can bind to the RNA polymerase and prevent it from functioning. I've been working on a prototype for this type of inhibitor, and I think it could work."

Emma smiled. "Let's get to work then."

Over the next few days, Emma, Tom and Daniel worked tirelessly to refine the small molecule inhibitor. They tested it on cells infected with the virus and saw promising results. The inhibitor was able to stop the virus from replicating without harming the host cells.

Excited by their progress, Emma, Tom and Daniel shared their findings with the rest of the team. Everyone was thrilled at the prospect of finally having a cure for the pandemic.

As the team got to work, Emma felt a sense of relief wash over her. She had been fighting the pandemic for months, and now, finally, they had a real chance of stopping it.

Tom and Daniel stood in the lab, staring at the computer screen displaying the results of the first successful cure. They had been waiting anxiously for the past few days for the test results, and now that they had arrived, they couldn't believe their eyes.

"It's a success," Daniel said, a broad smile spreading across his face. "The virus is completely gone from their systems."

This news excited every other member. They had been working tirelessly for weeks, and finally, their hard work had paid off. They knew there was still a long road ahead, but this was a significant milestone.

The team quickly prepared to test the cure on a small group of infected individuals. Emma led the team to a nearby hospital where they had identified a group of patients willing to participate in the trial.

As they entered the hospital ward, they were greeted by a group of anxious patients, each suffering from the virus. They all suited up in protective gear, began administering the cure to the patients. They monitored them closely, checking their vital signs and taking regular blood samples.

Over the next few hours, the patients' conditions slowly began to improve. The coughing and fever subsided, and their breathing became less labored. The team watched with growing excitement, hopeful that this would be the cure they had been searching for.

After 24 hours, they ran a final set of tests and were thrilled to find that the virus had been completely eradicated from the patients' systems. Emma and her team couldn't contain their excitement as they shared the news with each other.

"We did it!" Emma exclaimed, throwing her arms around Daniel. "This is a huge breakthrough."

Emma turned to her team, a small smile on her face. "We did it. We found the cure."

Maria nodded, her expression serious. "But our work isn't done yet. We need to make sure that this cure gets to everyone who needs it."

"We'll need to work with governments and healthcare organizations to ramp up production and distribution," Sarah said.

Daniel smiled, looking proud of his team's accomplishment. "Yes, but we still have a long way to go. We need to start manufacturing the inhibitor in large quantities. We also need to run more tests to make sure it's safe and effective."

"Daniel and I will get started on the manufacturing process," Tom said.

Emma assented, knowing that they couldn't stop now. "We need to make sure this cure gets to everyone who needs it."

Sarah chimed in. “And we need to make sure that people trust the cure. We’ll have to work on messaging and education to combat any misinformation that may arise.”

Emma turned to her, impressed by hers insight. “Exactly. We need to make sure that everyone understands the importance of taking the cure.”

Maria placed a reassuring hand on Emma’s shoulder. “The game is end now.”

Epilogue

It had been over a year since Emma and her team had found the cure for the pandemic. As the world slowly began to recover, they reflected on their journey and the lessons they had learned.

"I still can't believe we did it," Emma said, looking around at her team.

"I know, it's surreal," Maria agreed, a small smile on her face.

Daniel nodded. "It was a long and difficult road, but we made it through."

They were gathered in a conference room at the headquarters of the WHO. The walls were covered with maps, charts, and graphs tracking the spread of the virus and the distribution of the cure.

"I think one of the most important things we learned is the power of collaboration," Emma said. "We couldn't have done this alone. It took a global effort to find the cure and distribute it to those in need."

Sarah nodded. "And we also learned the importance of adaptability. We had to constantly adjust our plans and strategies as the situation changed."

Tom chimed in. "And we learned that science and technology can be incredibly powerful tools for solving problems, but they can also be dangerous if they're not used responsibly."

Emma looked around the room, feeling proud of the work they had accomplished. "I think we also learned the importance of hope," she said. "There were times when it felt like we would never find the cure, but we never gave up. We always held onto the hope that we could make a difference."

As they continued to reflect on their journey, they received updates on the progress of the world's recovery. The number of cases and deaths had dropped significantly, and economies were beginning to bounce back. But they also knew that the world would never be the same. The pandemic had changed everything, and there were still many challenges to face.

"We have to keep pushing forward," Maria said. "We can't let this experience go to waste. We have to use what we've learned to make the world a better place."

Tom nodded. "And we have to make sure that we're prepared for the next crisis. Because there will be one. We have to be ready to face it together."

As they left the conference room, Emma felt a sense of optimism for the future. The pandemic had been a dark and difficult time, but it had also shown what humanity was capable of when we worked together. She knew that there would be more challenges ahead, but she was ready to face them with her team by her side. And she knew that as long as they held onto hope, they could overcome anything.

www.ingramcontent.com/pod-product-compliance
Lightning Source LLC
LaVergne TN
LVHW010105170826
845678LV00012B/2247

* 9 7 8 9 8 8 7 6 9 9 6 3 7 *